THE CURIOUS CALLING

A STORY OF FAITH, FAMILY, AND FORGIVENESS

THE CURIOUS GIFT
BOOK 2

PETER DEHAAN

The Curious Calling: A Story of Faith, Family, and Forgiveness

The Curious Gift, Book 2.

This book is a work of fiction. Any resemblance to actual persons, living or dead, actual companies or organizations, or actual events is purely coincidental.

Library of Congress Control Number: 2026906214

Published by Rock Rooster Books, Grand Rapids, Michigan

ISBNs: 979-8-88809-198-2 (ebook); 979-8-88809-199-9 (paperback)

Credits: Developmental editor: Julie Harbison; Copyeditor: Robyn Mulder; Cover design: Fanderclai Design; Author photo: Chelsie Jensen Photography

CONTENTS

1

THE UNEXPECTED PRESENT

Excited for the day ahead, Lily got ready for school, marveling at all that had happened to her in the past few weeks. Her life had done a 180, from mostly sucky to almost always good.

A knock on her door startled her. It was Madison, her surrogate sister and new best friend—actually her only best friend ever.

Madison extended a smartly wrapped gift to Lily. "It's a just-because present." Swathed in handmade paper held in place with fluffy pink yarn, it was the most beautiful gift Lily had ever held—not that she had received many presents in her life. In fact, she couldn't remember a single one prior to meeting Madison and coming to live with the

Monroes. Yet gifts and pleasant surprises were common in the Monroe household.

The package was about the size of a book. Lily bounced with excitement. *Could it be? No, it was too much to hope for. But maybe. Or maybe not.* Unable to contain herself any longer, Lily voiced her question. "Are you giving me your grandma's special book?"

Madison grinned. "You'll have to open it to find out."

Lily carefully untied the yarn that held the wrapping in place. Once loosened, she respectfully laid the handcrafted paper on her desk. The gift was indeed a book. But it wasn't the book she expected. It was a journal of sorts with a soft, chic cover. Lily wasn't sure if it was dark gray or black, but it looked classy. Though she'd heard of fancy diaries, she'd never seen one, let alone held one in her hands. An elegant, silver calligraphy gave the book's title: *How to Make a Difference in the Lives of Other People.*

"It's not what I expected," Lily said. "But it's beautiful. I just love it. Thank you!"

Madison scrunched her eyebrows. "That's not the book I wrapped."

Lily gave Madison a questioning glance.

"The title is right, but the book is wrong,"

Madison explained. "The book I wrapped was the book Gram left for me after she died. You've seen it many times."

"That's what you wrapped?" Lily asked.

"Yes, it had an old, worn leather cover with fancy gold-embossed script. The last entry in the book said, 'You don't need this anymore. Give it to someone important to you,' which is exactly what I did—or at least what I tried to do."

"So you intended to give me your grandmother's book, but it turned into something else. I don't know what to think."

"Me neither," Madison said. "But how that book worked was always a mystery to me. I guess there are more secrets to uncover."

Lily knew Gram's book well, almost as well as Madison. She turned to the last page to read the last entry. But the page was blank. Completely empty. She flipped through the book. Not a single word. Every page was a sea of white.

Though the appearance of the book confused her, Lily knew what she could hope to expect from it. She was excited. Beyond excited. With a delighted squeal, she lunged toward Madison and wrapped her arms tightly around her best friend. "This is such an amazing gift. Thank you. Thank you so much. I'll do everything it tells me to do, and I won't let you down. Promise."

"You're welcome," Madison said. "Maybe I should've waited to give it to you, but I was too excited and couldn't wait any longer. I hope it won't distract you from school."

"No problem," Lily said. "Give me a sec, and I'll be down for breakfast."

Madison nodded and pulled the door shut.

Having privacy, Lily spun around and leaned against the door, sliding down to plop on the floor. Lily pulled the book to her chest and closed her eyes. She knew this was when she should pray, but she still struggled with the whole idea of talking to God. Yes, she had heard Madison pray many times. It seemed normal to Madison and the Monroe family, but it still felt awkward to her.

Then she recalled Madison's words. "Praying to God is like talking with a friend."

But should she fold her hands? Sometimes Madison did, and other times she didn't. Should she close her eyes or keep them open? Sometimes Madison did, and other times she didn't.

In case they might be important, Lily did both. With hands folded and eyes closed, she inhaled slowly. She tried to picture God in her mind, not that she had any idea what he looked like. No one did. After a time, an image of a kind, older man appeared in her mind. He had a warm smile, open arms, and eyes that twinkled with affection.

"Dear God," Lily said as she began her hesitant but hopeful prayer. "Will you make this book work for me like it did for Madison? Please do a miracle thingy, and use it to tell me what to do." She had said what was on her mind, but she didn't feel as if she was finished. Then she remembered. "Oh yeah, I ask this in Jesus's name. Amen."

Lily opened her eyes and blew out to release some tension. She cradled the book in her hands and stared at the front cover. With equal parts belief and doubt, she opened it. There on the first formerly blank page was some text. It wasn't the elegant handwritten penmanship of Madison's grandmother. Instead, it was calligraphy, just like the title on the cover.

She silently read the words slowly, moving her lips as if pronouncing each word aloud. "Well done, Lily! You're off to a great start. Invite Madison to go with you as you journey through life with this book. I will be with you and bless you every step of the way. -Papa."

2

CHEER FOR SHEA

Brimming with expectation, Lily checked her book every chance she got for the next couple of days. Sometimes she peeked every ten minutes. Nothing. She grew anxious. The first message had appeared right away. Why wasn't there another one? Frustration bubbled inside her like a boiling pot ready to jiggle off its cover. *Is God mad at me?*

Though Madison had treated her version of the book with misgiving when she first got it, Lily didn't hesitate. She had seen how God had spoken to Madison through the book and witnessed all the good things that happened when Madison obeyed its instructions.

Lily was ready to receive her own messages. But there were none. *What am I doing wrong?*

Grateful that Madison hadn't asked about the book, Lily knew that eventually her best friend would. That moment came three days later during their drive to school. After backing out of the driveway, Madison shifted into drive, accelerated slowly, and asked the question Lily was braced to hear but not ready to answer. "Have you gotten any messages yet?"

Somberly, Lily shook her head. When she realized Madison had kept her focus on the road and hadn't looked at her, Lily answered. "Not a single word. Maybe I'm not good enough to make it work."

"Nonsense," Madison said. "It's not about being good enough. All you need is faith the size of a mustard seed, which, by the way, is pretty small. You got that and more."

"Then why isn't God speaking to me?"

"Here's an idea. Pray about it. But instead of asking God to send you a message, thank him for the message he will provide."

"That sounds backward to me . . . and kind of cocky," Lily said.

"It's faith. Believe and receive."

Lily glanced askance at Madison to make sure she was serious. She certainly looked like it. "Okay then. I'll do it." Lily closed her eyes and folded her hands, even though Madison had said it wasn't necessary. "Dear God, thank you for this book and talking to me through it. Give me faith to receive and help me obey." She opened her eyes and then quickly clamped them shut again. "In Jesus's name, Amen." When they fluttered open, she turned toward Madison. "Now what?"

"Open your book and expect to see a new message."

"I can't."

"You can."

Lily slowly blew out the tension building inside her chest. Her shoulders relaxed. Her eyes snapped shut. "Thank you, Lord." She opened her eyes and then the book. She gasped. "There's a new message!"

"Care to share?"

"It says, 'Cheer for Shea this afternoon.' What in the world does that mean?"

Madison shrugged. "Not a clue."

"Didn't you say she's on the robotics team?

Maybe we're—I mean, maybe I'm—supposed to cheer for her at the competition."

"First," Madison said, "we're in this together. Just like you helped me, I'm open to help you. Second, I think all the robotics competitions are on Saturdays. But we should check to make sure."

"I'll do that as soon as we get to school," Lily said.

"Or you can use your phone to check right now."

Lily giggled. "Oops. I forgot I could do that. I've only had this thing for like a week." She pulled out her phone and began swiping and tapping. "Yep! You're right. No robotics today."

"It must be something else," Madison said.

"Could *cheer for her* mean to encourage her?" Lily asked. "Maybe we should check on how she and Ryan are doing."

"Good idea," Madison said. "But let's focus on the word *cheer* a bit more. What else is happening today?"

Lily pulled up the school's calendar. "There's a women's varsity basketball game right after school, but I'm sure Shea's not on the team."

"She doesn't seem like the athletic type," Madison said, "but let's double-check. Maybe the former goth girl is also a jock, as well as a techno geek."

Lily poked at her phone some more. "Bingo! It says she's a point guard—whatever that means."

"I think it's like the playmaker. She moves the ball up the court and then directs the plays. She must be good."

"The game starts half an hour after school gets out," Lily said. "Do you think we can stay for it? We're not scheduled to work."

"Let's plan on it."

Later that morning, Lily and Madison met Shea on the way to lunch. "How are things going with you and Ryan?" Lily asked.

"He's so dreamy." Shea gave a contented little purr. "Ever since our date last week, we've been hanging out every chance we get." She beamed, but her face soon clouded.

"What's wrong?" Lily asked.

"He wants to go to my game tonight, but I don't want him to," Shea said.

"Why not?" Lily asked.

"I won't play. I'll ride the bench the entire game."

"Aren't you the point guard?" Lily asked.

"Third string. Coach doesn't like me. I practice hard and put in extra time, but I've not played a single second the entire season."

"Maybe tonight will be different," Madison said.

Shea shook her head. "Doubt it. Bree twisted her ankle during practice, so that effectively makes me second string tonight. But it still won't make a difference."

"We're planning on coming to the game too," Lily said.

Shea groaned.

"We want to support you any way we can, whether or not you play," Madison added.

Shea looked up at the two girls. "Can I talk you out of it?"

Lily shook her head. "I think we're supposed to be there."

Shea gave her head a thoughtful bobble. "You and Madison do some strange things, but they've always worked out for me." After another pause, she gave a decisive nod to confirm. "Okay then.

You can go to the game. And if Ryan shows up, will you keep him company?"

"I'll be there," Ryan said as he shuffled up to join the trio. "You have my full support too." His hand found Shea's, and their sides sucked together like magnets.

Shea tipped her head onto his shoulder and purred again. "You're the best."

3

BE A DIFFERENCE MAKER

When school got out, Lily and Madison went straight to the cafeteria. They sat at a table and dove into their homework. Once finished, they hustled off to the gymnasium, arriving just as the warmup time was winding down.

Lily sat next to Ryan, with Madison next to her. "Thanks for keeping me company," he told them.

"We're here to cheer for Shea," Lily said, "whether or not she plays. But we hope she will."

"We want to encourage her," Madison added.

With the team in playoff contention, fans packed the place—even more so because they were playing their biggest rival. The visitor's section was nearly as full as the home side.

Lily cupped her hands around her mouth and called out to Shea. "Don't be a benchwarmer. Be a difference-maker!"

Though Shea didn't look at Lily, she grinned. A ball bounced her way. She picked it up, dribbled once, and shot a three-pointer from the top of the key. Swoosh. Nothing but net. She pumped her fist and sank another three-pointer. As she released her third shot, the buzzer sounded to signal the end of warmups. It went in too. Three for three. Shea turned to face Lily and grinned. She mouthed the words *thank you* and brought her fist to her chest. With another fist pump, she jogged toward the bench. With head back and a spring in her steps, she pranced off the court like a proud show horse.

From the start, the game was aggressive. Cheerleaders cheered, fans roared, and players competed. Despite being called for foul after foul, the ballers persisted in their hostile rivalry. Each whistle seemed to only encourage their contentious play.

As Shea had expected, she rode the bench, sitting on the far end.

By halftime, the score was tied, but most of the home team was in foul trouble.

Buoyed by their fans, the visiting team began the third quarter full of energy and overflowing with confidence. Not so for their rivals.

By the start of the fourth quarter, half the home team had fouled out, and they were down by ten points. When the point guard committed her final foul, Lily saw the coach glance at her bench. Only Bree and Shea were left. "Put me in," Bree mouthed to the coach.

Though she dashed onto the court, within a couple of plays she began limping, a little at first and then more noticeably. When the coach beckoned her, Bree shook her off. "I can do it." But she couldn't.

The other team saw Bree as the weak link and guarded her aggressively, blocking passes, stealing the ball, and pressing hard. One player pressed too hard and was called for a flagrant foul. In anger, she gave Bree a mighty shove. Bree fell backward and tumbled to the floor, writhing in pain. Though the official ejected the other player, Bree needed to be carried off the court.

The coach looked at Shea and grimaced. With a resigned shrug, she signaled Shea to go in. Most of the hometown fans groaned. But not Lily. She leapt to her feet and screamed. "You go girl. You got this!"

Ryan jumped up and hollered. "Go Shea!"

So did Madison. "You can do this!"

Lily again cupped her hands around her mouth. "Be a difference-maker!"

Shea nodded as she stepped to the line to shoot Bree's two foul shots. She drilled both, shortening the deficit to eight.

Then an alert Shea darted forward to intercept the inbound pass. She turned and sank a soft jumper for two more.

"Go Shea!" Lily screamed. "Go Shea!" Ryan and Madison joined Lily the second time. Lily spun around and encouraged the fans to join her. "Go Shea! Go Shea! Go Shea!" She accented each cheer with a mighty fist pump into the air. Soon she had the entire group of hometown fans cheering for Shea.

The visiting team struggled to advance the ball down the court, but eventually they did. As their point guard set up the next play, Shea lunged forward and stole the ball. She sped down the court and made an easy layup. They were now only down by four.

Encouraged by Shea, her team played harder,

mounting an impenetrable defense. The other team responded. For the next several minutes both teams struggled to move the ball up the court. No one scored.

With a minute left and still down by four, Shea moved the ball across mid-court to the top of the key. She faked left, she faked right, and then she gave a head fake to the net. The girl guarding her leapt high to block a shot that never happened. Shea dribbled to her left and then took the shot without opposition. It hit the rim, bounced around a bit, and eased through the net. They were now down by two, but time was running out.

Amid the roar of the crowd, the visitors inbounded the ball, moved it up the court, and tried to set up a final shot. They couldn't. As the shot clock wound down, the forward made a desperation attempt. It hit the rim and bounced harmlessly away and into the outstretched hands of Shea's teammate, who passed it to her.

Shea glanced at the clock as she allowed her teammates to get set for the game's final shot. With five seconds left, she made a bounce pass to the center and then took three steps back, behind the three-point line.

The defense collapsed around the center.

Instead of pivoting to do a skyhook—which she was renowned for—she passed the ball back to an unguarded Shea. Just as in warmups, Shea dribbled once and took her shot. Like before, the ball swished through the net, right as the buzzer went off.

4

TWO WINS

The ref signaled a good basket and held up three fingers. The scoreboard flashed the update, with the team winning by one. The crowd erupted with shouts of joy and flooded onto the court, cheering, jumping, and celebrating with unrestrained glee.

Lily hung back to watch the festivities, marveling at what had just happened. Madison and Ryan stood on either side of her.

Madison edged toward Lily. "I'd say your first assignment was a brilliant success! Let's count it as a win for you too."

"I just encouraged her and cheered," Lily said. "The success all belongs to Shea."

"Don't forget that you prayed too," Madison countered.

"You mean, *we* prayed," Lily corrected. "I still struggle with this praying thing. I doubt God heard my prayers, but I'm sure he heard yours."

"That's not how I see it. Don't doubt yourself just because you're new in your faith."

Ryan moved closer to Lily, confusion covering his face. "You mean you prayed for Shea to win the game?"

Lily shook her head. "Our prayer was that she'd be able to play. That's the prayer God answered."

"Either way, it was epic," Ryan said.

That's when Shea rushed up. She wrapped her arms around the trio. "I'm so glad you were here. Thanks for all your support." Tears of joy flowed from her eyes, trickling down her cheeks. "I'll never forget what you guys did. Especially you, Lily. Thank you." Giving them a parting hug, Shea whirled around and dashed off to join her exuberant teammates.

The girls said goodbye to Ryan and walked toward Madison's car. "I think Shea scored the last eleven points of the game," Lily said.

"And I don't think she missed a single basket,"

Madison added. "That means she shot 100 percent tonight."

"It also means she's shooting 100 percent for the season," Lily said.

On the way home, the pair continued gushing about the game and how Lily's book had prompted her to cheer for Shea.

"God works in amazing ways," Madison said.

"For sure," Lily said. "Though it still confuses me."

As they pulled up to the house, Madison's phone rang. She stopped the car at the curb and answered. "What's up?" She glanced at Lily. "It's work," she mouthed.

Madison looked away and spoke into the phone. "I can . . . Just me? . . . I understand . . . About 15 minutes . . . See you soon. Bye."

Madison glanced back to Lily. "I need to go in to work, but they only need one of us. Sorry."

"No worries," Lily said. "It's all good." She paused and then grinned. "Be a difference-maker!"

Lily got out of the car and walked to the front door. She waved goodbye as Madison drove away.

Madison's parents sat at the table, waiting for the girls for dinner. Lily jerked to a halt and looked at the floor. "Sorry, guys. We should've let you know we were running a bit late. Madison just got called in for work, so you're stuck with me tonight."

"That just means extra time with you," Madison's dad said. "By the way, I'm remiss for not doing this sooner, but you need to have your own house key." He handed her a key and keychain, complete with a personalized name tag. It said *Lily* in big fancy letters. Lily flipped it over. The other side said, "Make a difference wherever you go. Matthew 5:16."

"This is perfect, Dad," Lily said. "And thanks for the house key too. You guys are the best!"

5

A MENTOR

After a delicious meal and spending precious time with her new mom and dad, Lily offered to clear the table and do the dishes, even though tonight wasn't her turn. She wanted to give back, to do whatever she could to say thanks for taking her into their home and embracing her as family. She so didn't deserve it, and it really amazed her.

With the last of the dishes dried and put away, Lily prayed for courage. She had another instruction in her book to deal with—one she hadn't told Madison about. She was afraid to, worried that Madison might be mad . . . or worse. The last thing she wanted to do was damage her relationship with her new best friend.

It was also a confusing message. Even after looking up the word *mentor*, Lily still wasn't quite sure about it. But the notebook said to do it, so she would. At least she would try. That was her plan.

Trembling, Lily shuffled into the living room, Madison's mom sat on the couch reading her Bible. Not wanting to interrupt, Lily edged back. *I'll just ask later, when the timing is better.*

Madison's mom looked up, scrutinizing Lily. "What's up?" She closed her Bible.

Lily hesitated, searching for the right words. Not finding any, she just blurted out her book's instruction. "Will you mentor me?"

Joy burst from Mrs. Monroe's face. That was exactly the reaction Lily had hoped for, even though she feared it wouldn't happen.

"I'd be honored to." She jumped up and enveloped Lily, squeezing her tight. "I've been praying for an opportunity to help guide you into womanhood."

After several seconds, Lily patted Madison's mom's back twice. They pulled away and gazed into each other's eyes. The woman's eyes were misty.

"There are two ways I can mentor you," Mrs.

Monroe said. "The first is to be intentional about us doing life together."

Lily wrinkled her nose. "Like, to hang out?"

"Precisely."

"What would that look like?"

"For example, we could go grocery shopping together. That would give me a great opportunity to teach you about meal planning, nutrition, and getting the best value from what we buy."

Lily chuckled. "I've never thought about any of those things. Whenever I bought food, my only thought was filling my stomach for the least amount of money."

Mom laughed. "Let me guess, you ate a lot of ramen noodles."

"For sure." Lily's eyes sparkled. "I'm glad you never made them."

"And I never will."

Lily thought about that. Understanding flickered across her face. "Got it."

"Good. That's your first lesson." Her mentor grinned. "The other way to mentor you is to look at what Scripture teaches, specifically about womanhood."

"But when would we do it?"

"Madison is a morning person. You and I are

not. Perhaps some evenings when you're not working and you have your homework done, we could spend a few minutes looking at what the Bible can teach us."

"Can we start tonight?" Lily asked.

Mrs. Monroe sat on the couch and patted the cushion next to her. "Let's read the story of Ruth."

6

ZERO FOR THREE

After talking with Madison's mom, Lily retreated to her room. Mrs. Monroe's eagerness to mentor Lily filled her with joy. At least that's what she thought it was. Joy was a new idea to her, something she had never experienced.

Even though Madison's older brother, Michael, had never met her, he had willingly given up his room for her. A quick phone call to thank him turned into a longer conversation, and they'd repeated it almost every night since. Some nights he only had time for a quick text, but usually they enjoyed a lengthy video call.

She was falling for him and hoped he felt the same way about her. She thought he did. In fact, she was quite sure, with only a sliver of doubt. He always contacted her every night. Tonight they planned to talk at nine. She glanced at the senior picture she had found of him and placed on her dresser. She gave his image a dreamy smile and let out a contented sigh.

Lily completed her homework much faster than she expected. Leaving plenty of time before Michael would call, she wondered what to do. With Madison's warning prominent in her thoughts, Lily knew to not let herself get sucked into wasting time with mindless activity on her phone. She considered going downstairs to watch some TV but decided to check her book to see if there were any more instructions.

She opened it.

An elegant calligraphy message filled the next page with three oversized words. "Well done, daughter!" The next page continued: "You just set Shea's life on a different trajectory."

Lily envisioned God up in heaven smiling down on her, like a proud papa beaming over the accomplishments of a beloved child. Her Lord's esteem flooded into her being.

Her heavenly Father loved her, and he approved. Lily allowed her eyes to flutter closed.

She couldn't have hoped for anything more. That's what mattered more than anything. She could live in this moment forever and wanted to never forget it. "Thank you, Papa," she whispered. She folded her hands and bowed her head, assuming a prayer posture. But it wasn't to ask for anything. It was to listen.

In that instant, God's affirmation permeated her. Lily had never felt so loved. Never ever. She squeezed her eyes tight, and tears trickled out, cascading down her cheeks and falling into her lap.

She didn't know whether seconds had passed or if it was minutes, but at last she opened her eyes, smearing the tears of joy across her cheeks. She didn't care what she looked like.

Lily let out a contented sigh and turned the page in her notebook.

She shuddered, slamming it shut. "No!" Clamping her eyes tight, Lily inhaled deeply as she sought to regain her composure. She considered trying to pray about it but doubted it would do any good.

Lily opened the book again and reread the message. "Visit your mom in prison." Lily shook her head. *No way. No how.* She crossed out the message with a bold X and then added her own in block letters. "NO!"

But the facing page had another message. "Surprise Michael."

She turned the page to see if there was more. There was. It said, "Apply for a credit card."

Lily considered her options. She did the last one first. Already having a checking and savings account, it was an easy step to apply for a credit card online. She filled in the information and clicked submit. Immediately, an email arrived confirming they had received her request and were processing it.

She was still considering how to surprise Michael when a follow-up email came. *That was fast.* But her excitement vanished as she read the message. "We are sorry, but due to your poor credit history, we must decline your request for a credit card at this time. We encourage you to take steps to restore your credit before reapplying."

Lily would have understood if they told her she had no credit, but to say she had bad credit surprised her. Until a few weeks ago, she'd never even had a bank account. The extent of her financial dealings revolved around whatever little cash she had in her pocket.

Having eliminated the idea of visiting her mom and striking out at getting a credit card, that left the final task of surprising Michael. Since he always called her, she'd surprise him tonight by taking the initiative. That would show him she was interested and willing to do her part in building their relationship.

Lily checked the mirror, brushed her hair, and practiced her smile. She wanted to make sure the first image he saw of her tonight would grab his attention. Ready, she pulled up his contact information and pressed the video icon.

It rang for a long time, and at last he answered.

Only it wasn't him.

It was some woman. "Michael's phone." She slurred her words. Loud music blasted over the phone, and multiple competing conversations made it hard for Lily to hear. "This is . . . ah . . . his answering service." The woman gave an uneasy giggle.

Lily chose to ignore all this and be mature. "Is Michael available?"

"He must be here somewhere," the woman said. "I just saw him like a few seconds ago. Who are you? His little sister?"

"No," Lily said. Irritation rose within her. "I'm his . . . I'm his girlfriend."

The woman laughed. "That's so sweet. Bless your little heart. But just to let you know, Missy, I'm his girlfriend. Don't mess with me."

"No," another voice screamed. Her head bobbed into view behind the first woman. "I saw him first. He's all mine. As soon as he gets back with my drink, he'll set you both straight!" As the two tussled, the phone fell to the floor.

All Lily saw was a sea of legs. She disconnected the call and fell onto her bed for a good cry.

She still lay there whimpering at nine when her phone rang. She didn't answer.

7

HE'S HISTORY

With a huff, Lily rolled over in bed. She squinted at the clock. 3:07. Only five minutes had passed since the last time she looked. Was she getting any sleep at all? Haunted by Michael's betrayal, Lily's raging emotions swung back and forth between anger and hurt.

How could I have been so wrong about him?

She thought he was different. That she could hope to have a happily-ever-after life with him. But nope. He was a player just like every other guy—just like the father she never knew.

Lily repositioned her pillow to try to find a dry spot. No use.

If she couldn't trust him with her heart, should she trust him with any of the things he taught her about God, faith, and the Bible?

No. If he was a phony with his relationships, was everything he had told her a lie? Possibly. Probably. For sure. She decided to reject everything about him.

Is this a case of "like father, like son"?

Maybe she couldn't trust Dad either. Maybe she had given her heart to him too quickly, hoping in vain he could be the father she never knew. What about Mom? Maybe her own mother wasn't so bad after all. Maybe she should visit her in jail and try to make the best of their dysfunctional relationship. But she didn't want to do that either.

Lily knew she should pray. She knew that's what Madison would tell her to do. But she didn't. She couldn't and didn't know what to say. Besides, she doubted it would do any good anyway.

She rolled over with a heavy sigh and clamped her eyes shut. More tears leaked out. She didn't care. She welcomed them.

At last, her alarm went off. Lily stumbled out of bed, her morose mood propelling her into the day. Seeing Michael's photo on her dresser angered her.

Stop staring at me, you loser. She suppressed the urge to chuck his stupid picture across the room. That would be disrespectful to the Monroes and noisy too. Instead, she grabbed it from its perch and shoved it face down in the back of the bottom drawer, under an old pair of jeans.

She peeked at her book, not that she cared anymore anyway. More instructions. Yuck!

Lily shuffled through her morning routine, ate breakfast in silence, and tumbled into Madison's car as they headed off to work. Maybe an eight-hour shift at Citrus City would take her mind off her sorry, pathetic life.

If only Madison would let her wallow in self-pity. But Lily suspected her best friend wouldn't allow her to self-destruct. In fact, she knew it. Even though she couldn't trust Michael anymore and needed to be cautious with Mom and Dad, Madison was the real deal. Her faith mattered and directed everything she said and did.

Lily knew she could count on Madison, even if she couldn't count on anyone else. Oh, and there was God too. But Lily needed Madison's help if she had any hope of growing in her newfound faith.

They'd just set off on their trek to work when

Madison did exactly what Lily expected. "Want to talk about it?"

"No!"

"It might help."

"It won't," Lily sputtered. "And don't tell me to pray about it either."

"When we don't have the words to pray, the Holy Spirit groans for us. You can be sure he's doing that for you right now."

"Groans for us?" Before Madison could explain more, Lily waved her hand. "Whatever."

"I expected you'd still be celebrating the win yesterday afternoon . . . both for the team and for the brilliant way you obeyed God's instructions in your notebook."

"That's yesterday's news. Frankly, I'm fed up with that stupid book. It doesn't work. It just causes problems."

"Don't you remember? That book caused problems for me when I had it," Madison said. "Like going on a date I didn't want to go on, getting detention, and having Shea nearly assault me."

"But everything worked out."

"And it will for you too."

Lily shook her head. "Not a chance."

"Tell me about it."

"There were a lot of new instructions last night." Lily inhaled deeply before continuing. "First, it congratulated me for cheering on Shea. But then it told me to visit my mom in prison. No way. Then it said apply for a credit card, but I was denied. Strike two . . ."

"And strike three?"

"I don't want to talk about it. I don't want to talk about *him*."

"Michael?"

"Yes! That two-timing, double-crossing phony."

Lily glanced at Madison, just in time to see her clench her jaw. "Tell me what happened." Her carefully controlled words emerged with tight precision.

"The other instruction was to surprise Michael. I surprised him all right, but it wasn't a good one. He was at some raging party. I talked to his girlfriend."

"First," Madison said, "Michael doesn't do parties. He's there to get an education, and nothing will distract him from that. Second, Michael doesn't drink."

"Doesn't drink?" Lily asked.

Madison shook her head. "No one in our family does."

"Seriously?"

"It's expensive and only causes problems."

"Okay then," Lily said. "No parties and no drinking."

"Third," Madison continued, "he doesn't have a girlfriend . . . at least not one in college."

"I talked to her! I talked to two of them! They're older than me and better looking. It was stupid to think I'd ever have a chance with him. He probably just sees me as a little girl."

"Michael and I are close." Madison said. "I know he likes you. He really likes you."

"If he did, he wouldn't be running around with other women. Then he tried calling me at nine, just like we planned, as if nothing had happened."

"Did you talk to him?"

"No way! Fool me once, shame on you. Fool me twice, shame on me."

"Did he try texting you?"

"Like about twenty times," Lily said. "First, he pretended nothing had happened. Then he acted all worried, as if he cared. His last message said he was praying for me . . . that I was okay."

"Did you tell him you were?"

"Of course not! I don't owe him anything. Especially after how he disrespected me and broke my heart."

"I'm sure he has a good explanation," Madison said. "But you'll need to talk to him to find out what it is. Do it right away. Like on your first break."

"Not going to happen. He's history."

"I don't think you really mean that."

"But I do."

8

THE DRIVER'S LICENSE

True to her word, Lily didn't reach out to Michael during her first break, even though he had resumed texting her. His last pathetic text sounded desperate. "Please, Lily. We need to talk. I don't want to lose you."

When Madison later tried to talk about Michael, Lily changed the subject. "I had a new instruction in my book this morning. It said, 'Get your driver's license.' Will you help me with that?"

"There are a bunch of hoops to jump through to get your license," Madison said.

"All done," Lily said. "I just need to take my road test. And I need a car for that."

"Have you logged all your practice hours?"

"My mom signed off on it before she was arrested."

"But did you actually do it? I didn't know your mom had a car."

"She doesn't. The bank repoed it last year. But before she lost it, I drove a lot. I've been driving since I was like thirteen."

"Thirteen?"

"Had to. Mom had been arrested, and I drove to the police station to post her bond."

"You mean you illegally drove to the police station? That was gutsy."

"Well, first I had to drive to get her bail money. Then I went to the station." Lily studied Madison's face. She needed to sell it. "I'm a really good driver."

Madison inhaled slowly. "Let me think about it."

Lily ignored Michael during her lunch break too. Instead, she hung out with Jason, who had shown up to spend time with Madison during her lunch. The afternoon got busy, and Lily skipped her last break so she wouldn't have to think about Michael. But she couldn't stop.

Apparently, neither could Madison. "I let Michael know you were okay," Madison said to Lily during a brief lull that afternoon. "He had been worried you'd been hurt or even . . . dead."

"Like he cares."

"But he does. More than you realize. Much more," Madison said. "If you won't talk to him for his sake, will you at least do it for mine? Tonight?"

Lily let out a slow sigh. "Okay. But only because you asked me to, not because I want to." She pulled out her phone to text him. "I'm willing to talk tonight. You pick the time, but no girlfriends."

"I don't have any girlfriends," Michael texted back. "But if you'll let me, I'd like to change that."

Lily typed a snarky reply but deleted it before she made the mistake of sending it. Instead, she texted, "How about 8:30?"

He agreed. "Can't wait."

After work, the girls walked to Madison's car. Madison acted oddly. Lily wondered if Madison was thinking about Michael. Though she herself had tried not to, she certainly was. When they reached the car, Madison turned to face Lily, giving her a thoughtful gaze.

At last, Madison smiled. She extended her arm and handed Lily the keys. "Let's drive around the parking lot a bit, away from other cars. If you do a good job, I'll let you drive home."

Lily did—both a good job driving around the parking lot and at driving home.

As the girls walked to the front door of her house, Madison turned to Lily. "Even though this is your assignment, let me ask Dad about you using our car to take your test."

"Thanks," Lily said. "I was worried about what to say."

"Dad isn't a scary guy," Madison said. "No worries."

They found him in the kitchen preparing dinner. Though Madison's mom usually did the cooking during the week, Saturday was her dad's turn. He perked up when the girls arrived. "I'm pulling out all the stops tonight," he said. "We're having baked lasagna."

"Your lasagna is the best, Dad," Madison said.

"Lily is ready to get her driver's license. Is it okay for her to use our car to take her road test?"

Madison's dad didn't react at first, continuing to place the last of the lasagna noodles in the pan. At last he looked up. "I'm certainly open to that," he said. "But first she needs to log her hours, and before that, we need to add her to our insurance."

Lily's heart thumped as she glanced at Madison. Though her mother had signed off on the hours, Lily hadn't driven a single one. How could she? Their car had already been repossessed, so there had been no car for her to drive. Logging the hours for real wouldn't be a problem, but she hadn't even thought about having insurance.

For her part, Madison's eyes popped open in shock. "She needs to be on our insurance policy to drive our car?"

"Technically, yes," Dad said. "Though it might be okay to have someone else drive our cars occasionally, because Lily lives with us, I'm sure the insurance company will insist we add her to our coverage. But since we're not adding another vehicle, it shouldn't cost too much more—at least I hope not. I'll take care of it on Monday. Then we can start logging her hours. Before we know it, she'll have her license."

Lily glanced at Madison, waiting nervously to see what she would say. Would she confess, or would she keep Lily's driving a secret?

Though Lily had never cared too much in the past about whether it was legal for her to drive her mom's car or not, she cared very much about whether she could drive Madison's. Despite her irrational thoughts earlier this morning about whether her new dad was trustworthy, she knew in her heart that he was. And she certainly didn't want to do anything to disappoint him.

Lily inhaled deeply to come clean, but Madison made a slight gesture to stop her.

"Dad," Madison said, "I messed up. I let Lily drive our car home from work this afternoon, but it was just this once. I'm sorry. It won't happen again. Promise."

Madison's dad turned to face her. "Aside from being illegal, that was a huge error in judgment," he said. "But I'll grant you grace, especially since your motivation to help Lily was honorable. As they say, 'no harm, no foul.' But I need you both to promise me it won't happen again until after I have the insurance taken care of."

"Agreed." Madison rushed forward and gave her dad a huge hug.

Lily was even more grateful, sorry for the negative thoughts she had had about her new dad this morning. She hurried forward too and wrapped her arms around them both. She whispered in his ear, "Thank you so much, Dad. I love you."

9

IDENTITY THEFT

Tonight was Lily's turn to clean up after dinner and do the dishes. It was mindless activity that gave her alone time to think. *That's a good thing, isn't it?* But all she could think about was Michael, that weasel of a guy. She pushed down the little remaining affection she had toward him and let negativity overtake her thoughts.

Why did I ever let Madison convince me to talk to him tonight? There's nothing he can say or do that could change a thing. Yet deep down, she hoped he would.

Then she made the mistake of peeking at her stupid book. Another instruction. *Grr.* "Listen to Michael. Keep an open mind." She slammed it shut but resisted the urge to chuck it in the trash.

Still steaming, she put away the last of the clean dishes.

Mr. Monroe walked into the kitchen. He wore a determined look.

Lily attempted perky. “What’s up, Dad?”

“I hope you don’t mind, but Madison told me about you applying for a credit card.”

Lily held her breath. *Am I in trouble?* She knew Dad could be stern when needed, but so far, she’d never seen it directed at her. She’d always been on his good side and wanted to keep it that way. *Maybe I shouldn’t have applied for it after all.*

“I applaud your desire to establish credit,” he said. “I hope that will help you learn good financial responsibility. But Madison says you were denied for bad credit. Perhaps I can help.”

Lily slowly released the pent-up air inside her lungs. She wasn’t in trouble after all. *What a relief.* “I expected they’d say I had no credit. So it was a shock to hear that I had bad credit. What should I do?”

“If you want, we can go online and access your credit reports. You can get a free copy each year, one from each of the three credit bureaus. Once we study the reports, it should give us an idea of how to move forward. Shall we do that?”

"Yes, please."

"Let's go to my office, and I'll walk you through it."

Thirty minutes later, Lily had her three credit reports. "I don't understand," she told Dad. "They each list the last two places we've lived, and this business is where we buy all our furniture. But why are they listing me as being in default?"

"According to this, they say you were renting furniture and not buying it. When you were evicted and the furniture was unrecoverable, they reported you in default for the entire amount."

"My mom said she bought the furniture, but I always wondered where she got the money. Now it all makes sense."

Mr. Monroe sighed. "It looks like you've been the victim of identity theft."

"But why would anyone do that to me?"

"Unfortunately, I suspect your mother did it, likely because her credit was too bad. She could trade on yours for a time."

Anger roiled inside Lily. Once again, she saw what a rotten parent her biological mother had been. *I'll never visit you now. And I'll never forgive you!*

"Let me make a phone call tomorrow to a friend I have on the police force. I think he'll be able to set us in the right direction. It's Detective Brindle. We go to church with him. I'll let you know what he advises, and then I'll work with you to get this resolved."

"Thanks, Dad," Lily said. "I don't know what I'd do without your help."

"Just be aware that even if we get this resolved, Mom and I will probably need to cosign for your credit card, just like we did for Madison. But if we do, we'll hold you to the same expectations we have for her."

"Understood," Lily said. "I wouldn't have it any other way."

10

MICHAEL'S STORY

Lily checked the time. Eight twenty. She shifted in her chair at Dad's desk and turned to look up at him. "Is there anything else? I have an important phone call I need to make in ten minutes."

"Michael?"

Lily looked suspiciously at Dad. "Ahh, yes. How did you know?"

"There will be no need to call him tonight."

"Why? Though I don't really want to, I promised Madison I would."

"I understand Michael's on his way here to see you in person." Dad also checked the time. "In fact, I suspect he's already arrived."

Lily jumped from her chair and bounced, glee

beaming from her face. "Really!" Then she tempered her response, remembering that she was mad at him for cheating on her. "Oh, really?"

"You two can talk in the den. Let's go see if he's here."

Fear surged through Lily as she followed Dad. She struggled to control her breathing. Though she willed her pulse to slow down, it didn't. Her stomach rumbled with anxiety, and she wiped her suddenly sweaty hands on her pants. *Father God,* she prayed silently, *please show me what to say and do when I talk with Michael. Please work everything out. I asked this in Jesus's name. Amen.*

Mr. Monroe ushered Lily into the den. He partially closed the door, leaving it ajar. "We'll grant you a degree of privacy, but the door stays open." Then he left.

There sat Michael on the loveseat. He jumped up when he saw her. "I'm so glad to know you're okay." He took a step toward her and extended his arms. "It's so good to finally see you in person."

Lily slowly shook her head as she scooted to the recliner. She gave him a firm stare, as if commanding him not to come closer. His joy at seeing her washed from his face. He returned to the loveseat with a grim expression.

She sat. So did he.

They stared at each other.

At last, he broke the silence. "I'm not sure what the problem is, but I sensed I needed to see you in person if I had any hope of making things right."

"I doubt you can," Lily said. The words came out matter-of-factly, with no hint of emotion—or affection.

"Just tell me what's wrong," he said. "I'll do whatever I can to fix it. Anything."

"Though we never talked about our relationship," Lily said at last, "I assumed there was an understanding. That's why I allowed myself to fall for you. That was a mistake. You played me. You cheated on me. You broke my heart, and I'll never forgive you."

Though she wanted to cry over how much he had hurt her, Lily clamped her jaw tight and willed her tears to remain dammed up behind her eyes.

Shock covered Michael's face. "I don't know what you're talking about. I didn't play you. And I didn't cheat on you." He gulped. "I . . . I really like you. A lot."

"That's not what your girlfriend told me."

"My girlfriend? I don't have a girlfriend . . . except for you . . . at least, I hope so."

"Actually, it's girl*friends*," Lily retorted. "I talked to them both at the party last night."

"But I don't go to parties," Michael said. "I'm in college to learn and don't waste my time on meaningless distractions."

"I wanted to surprise you and called around seven," Lily explained. "Your girlfriend answered your phone and mocked me. Then your other girlfriend popped into view and said she was your real one. Then the two of them started fighting."

Michael slowly shook his head. "I have no idea what you're talking about." He closed his eyes and lowered his head.

Lily wasn't sure if he was thinking or praying. But either way, it didn't matter. She was done with him.

Then Michael's eyes popped open and beamed. He looked at her. "I think I understand what happened. It's kind of a long story, so please give me time to explain everything. Okay?"

Lily didn't respond.

"Most everyone at college parties on Friday nights. Not me. It's a great time to study. There are three other guys in my study group. We go to the library every Friday evening. We have the place to ourselves.

"This week, two other guys asked to join us. I didn't want them to but felt it would be rude to say no. Then they said it would be more convenient for us to meet in their dorm room. We agreed. When we got there, they weren't really focused on studying. But we tried to anyway.

"After about twenty minutes, a couple more guys showed up, but they weren't the studious types. They turned our attempt at studying into a social gathering, which soon overflowed into the entire floor. I left then. That was about half-past six."

Lily shifted in her chair. So far it sounded plausible. But she waited to hear his explanation about his girlfriends.

Michael continued. "It wasn't until after I'd been back to my dorm room for an hour or so that I realized I didn't have my phone. I was in such a rush to leave that I must have left it in their dorm room. So I hustled back, and a full-on party was raging. I searched and searched. Eventually, I found it on the floor, underneath a futon. That was well after eight."

Lily allowed herself to relax a bit, as she held onto hope that his story would all check out.

"I hurried back to my dorm, just in time to call you at nine, as promised," Michael said. "But you didn't answer. At first, I assumed we had our times mixed up. I tried again and then a third time. Next, I started texting. Then I grew worried and was sure something bad had happened to you."

Michael shifted on the loveseat. "I thought about texting Madison to ask if you were all right, but by then it was after one in the morning, and I didn't want to wake her. That's when I started praying. I should have done that sooner." He looked at Lily, his eyes pleading for her to believe him.

She relaxed her posture but held back her smile. She needed to confirm things with him first. "So when I called you at seven, only your phone was at the party. You weren't. Is that correct?"

Michael nodded. "That's how I worked out the timeline."

"But who were the two women—the ones who claimed to be your girlfriends?"

Michael shook his head. "I have no idea. But I can assure you—I promise you—that there are no women in my life. At least none besides Mom, Madison . . . and you."

11

MICHAEL'S GOODBYE

Lily's deep despair from earlier on Saturday flipped into total bliss at Michael's explanation. She knew—she just knew—that he was a good man and that she could trust him. *But why did my emotions turn on him so quickly?*

The hours flew by. Saturday turned to Sunday. The five of them went to church, with Lily sitting next to Michael. When the minister announced the Scripture reading, Lily fumbled to find the passage. But Michael quickly turned to it and held his Bible for her to read. When Lily brought her hand up to steady it, their hands touched. Though it was by accident, neither pulled away. It was a magical moment for sure, but it so distracted Lily that she couldn't remember a single word of the text.

Next was Sunday lunch, which consisted of a tossed salad and warmed up lasagna. It was almost as good today as when it was fresh. Sunday afternoon family time followed the meal. It was a two-hour window to focus on each other without the intrusion of technology. With the sun shining brightly, they went for an extended stroll.

All too soon it was time for Michael to leave. Lily, Michael, and Madison walked to the car. Madison handed the keys to Michael. "Do you still remember how to drive?" Her eyes danced with mirth.

"Don't forget that this was my car long before it was yours." Michael got in the driver's side and began adjusting the seat and mirrors to accommodate his lengthy frame.

Lily reached for the handle of the backseat door, but Madison laid a hand on hers. "You sit up front with Michael."

"You sure?"

Madison smiled and nodded.

Lily beamed. "Thanks. Thanks a million."

With the three of them buckled, Michael eased the car forward to begin the two-and-a-half-hour trek back to the university. He was a careful driver, just like his dad. With him behind the wheel, Lily knew she'd be safe. In fact, she knew in her heart that she'd be safe with him whatever the situation. *Why, oh why, did I ever doubt him?*

Lily turned to him and asked a question she'd been wondering about. "Since you don't have a car and we're taking you back to college, how did you even get here last night?"

Michael laughed. "God provided." Then he explained. "The parents of a guy in my study group made a surprise visit to him on Saturday. It was a day trip, and I knew they'd be heading this way to get home. Dropping me off was a slight detour for them, but they were happy to help, even more so once they found out that my love life was on the line." He glanced at Lily and grinned.

"I'm glad they did." Then Lily's gleam turned to gloom. She gulped hard and sucked in a lungful of courage. "I'm so sorry I didn't trust you and reached the wrong conclusion. I should've known better. And I should've talked to you and let you straighten things out."

"No worries," he said. "This way I got to see you. That's a bonus. I was going crazy thinking I'd have to wait until spring break to meet you in person."

"Are you still coming home then?"

"Definitely. Sooner if I can work it in."

"Even if you can't, at least we can still talk each night."

In the silence that followed, Lily remembered Madison sitting alone in the backseat. She wanted to include her best friend in the conversation and not shut her out.

But before Lily could think what to say, Michael asked Lily a question. "What did you think of Pastor's message this morning?"

"I really liked it," Lily said. "I never thought about God adopting us into his family. It's so cool. Yet it's also hard for me to wrap my mind around."

"In this lifetime, we'll never understand everything there is to know about God," Michael said.

"Madison says the same thing," Lily responded. "I can't believe that I'm part of his family. It's grace . . . and mercy . . . and love all wrapped into one amazing gift of salvation through Jesus."

The three of them talked more about being part of God's family, about faith, and about the Bible. Lily's heart soared with gratitude and amazement. She was a child of God—his adopted daughter. She also had a boyfriend. And a best friend who pointed her to God and had connected her with Michael.

Her life today—filled with faith, expectation, and promise—was the exact opposite of what it had been only a few weeks earlier. God was at work in her life, and Madison was his instrument that made it happen.

The miles sped by and in no time at all—way too soon—they arrived at Michael's dorm.

Michael jumped out of the car and ran around to open the door for Lily. As he did, Madison moved to the front seat. This gave Lily a bit of alone time with Michael to say goodbye.

Lily looked up at him with adoration beaming from her face. Gazing into her eyes, he brushed the side of her cheek with the back of his hand. "You're amazing."

She held her breath, waiting for him to kiss her. He didn't. Instead, he gave her a sideways hug and patted her shoulder twice.

Then he walked away, leaving Lily totally confused. *If I'm so great, why not kiss me? Aren't I good enough for you?* In a daze, she slid into the passenger seat and pulled the door shut. "I'm not sure what just happened."

Madison looked at her. "What do you mean?"

"He said I was amazing, but he didn't kiss me. What's wrong with me?"

Madison chuckled. "Michael's a good guy, but he doesn't always say what he's thinking."

"All I wanted was a simple kiss to cap off the day. Is that too much to ask?"

"Michael wonders if the first kiss he gives his wife should be at their wedding," Madison said. "He thinks it would be powerful."

"He could've at least mentioned that and not left me hanging."

"Like I said, sometimes Michael doesn't say what he's thinking."

"But if he won't kiss me, how do I know he loves me?"

"That's simple," Madison said. "It's by how he treats you."

"You and Jason have kissed," Lily pointed out.

"We have, but I wonder if Michael's way isn't better. One kiss can lead to two, and that can lead to more, but I'm going to wait to have sex until I get married."

"What about Jason?"

"We haven't talked about it . . . but we should. We must."

"If my mother would've waited," Lily mused aloud, "I wouldn't be here today."

"Though good came from it," Madison said, "that doesn't make it right."

Lily needed to think about this. In fact, she had a lot to process. About kissing, about her fickle emotions, and about Michael. Then were the issues of forgiveness, her ruined credit, and her rotten mother. Yep, she had a lot to figure out. And she had the next two and a half hours to do just that.

12

SEEK TO SERVE

The first thing Lily had to wrestle with was her dramatic attitude shifts toward Michael. It shocked her to realize just how quickly she had turned from hot to cold and back to hot again. He deserved better, but she had no idea how to make sure she didn't do it again. In fact, she knew she would.

Maybe Madison could help.

"When I thought Michael had another girlfriend," Lily confessed, "I went berserk. I began thinking all sorts of crazy things about him. Mom and Dad too. I even thought about moving out. That's how deranged I was."

"I get it," Madison said. "Our girl emotions aren't bad, but we can't let them run wild."

"What do we do?"

"The Bible says to take every thought captive and make it obedient to Jesus."

"What in the world does that mean?" Lily asked.

"To control our thoughts and not let them control us. It's hard to do on our own, but God can help."

"That probably means praying about it, right?"

"Yep," Madison said. "It also means not thinking about what's bad and focusing on what's good."

"So instead of thinking Michael was a lying cheat, I should've focused on his good parts."

"Correct."

"Got it. But next time I mess up, will you remind me?"

"Only if you'll do the same thing for me," Madison said. "We don't want to give the enemy a foothold into our lives."

"The enemy?"

"You know, the devil. Satan. Lucifer."

"Got it."

Lily recapped this. *Think about good things, not bad. Pray about controlling my thoughts. And don't let the devil into my life.* That would be hard to do, but she had to try. And with God's help she'd work to do just that.

"Next," Lily said, "is that I've tried to do too many of my book's assignments on my own. I should have let you in on them . . . oh, and prayed about them too."

"Like what?"

"Trying to surprise Michael was a disaster. I bet you'd have had a different idea of what to do."

Madison grinned. "I'd have suggested sending him a gift. Next week is his birthday."

Lily groaned. "And you'd probably have known the right gift too."

"It's geeky, but he'd really like a Stirling engine kit."

"What in the world is that?" Lily asked.

"Look it up! Less expensive would be a physics-themed T-shirt, especially one about Einstein."

"What did you get him?"

"It's a hoodie that says, 'Why did the chicken cross the Mobius strip?'"

"What?" Lily thought for a moment and shrugged. "I give up. Why?"

"To get to the same side."

"I don't get it."

"It's a physics thing." Madison grinned. "Quite brilliant, actually."

"Maybe after he starts wearing it, he'll tell me what it means." Lily paused. "If I promise to pay you back, can I use your credit card to buy him a birthday present?"

"For sure."

Lily recalled some of her other instructions. "The book said to visit my mom in jail, but I'm not going to."

"It took me a while to realize I needed to do what the book said," Madison said. "It never worked out to waffle or debate God about it."

"You mean like visiting my mom?"

"Yep."

Lily shook her head.

"When I had the notebook," Madison said, "God told me to take you to see your mom. You didn't want to. But I think you should have done it anyway. Now you have a second chance."

"You may be right, but I'm not ready."

"Maybe you need to forgive her first," Madison said.

"I'll never forgive her."

"Never say never. You can do whatever you

need to do because God will give you the strength to do it. All you need to do is ask."

Lily made another mental note. *Always do what God says. Ask him for help when I don't want to do it . . . or am afraid.*

"Next," Lily said, "is today's instruction. It said, 'Seek to serve.' But I have no clue what that means."

"We need to serve others, just like Jesus did," Madison explained. "It helps point people to him." She paused. Then insight flickered across her face. "Since he gave you that instruction on Sunday, it might mean to do something at church."

Lily shrugged. "I suppose so."

"My family serves in a lot of areas. At least we did until Gram had her stroke. We took a break for a while to focus on healing from her passing. But I think we're ready to move back into serving. At least I am."

"How? Where?"

"Dad serves on the elder board and oversees church finances. Mom works in the nursery once a month and is the director of women's ministries. I teach third and fourth graders two Sundays a month and often greet the other weeks."

"But what about me?"

"What interests you? What are you passionate about?"

"I'm not passionate about anything," Lily said. "Until recently, my only thought was just making it through the day. I've never thought beyond that—until now."

"Then you can try different things and see what fits. Maybe serve with one of us."

"Being an elder or director is out," Lily thought aloud. "I have no idea how to deal with babies, and I don't see myself as a teacher. I guess that leaves greeting. What's that involve?"

"We stand at the main doors and welcome people when they arrive," Madison said. "It's simple: make eye contact, smile, and say hello. Some adults expect a handshake too. And boys get into fist bumps."

Lily nodded. If this was the best way for her to serve Jesus, she'd do it. "Can I greet with you?"

"Sure."

Though Madison was probably a natural at greeting, Lily knew it would stretch her. Then an idea came to her. "I'm not sure if this counts, but last Sunday the women's restroom was a mess. It was out of paper towels and the trash was overflowing. It seems silly, but can I serve Jesus by cleaning?

Cleaning isn't my passion, but working at Citrus City has shown me I'm good at it."

"Doing what no one else wants to do is a great way to serve Jesus," Madison said.

Tension left Lily's body as her tight shoulders relaxed. Her spirit soared like a kite lifted by the wind. "What do we need to do to make it happen?"

13

BEFRIEND BREE

When Lily arrived at school on Monday morning, Friday's epic basketball win seemed far away. Between then and now were her struggles in following God's instructions, her roller-coaster relationship ride with Michael, and added clarity from Madison. But the game was still what everyone else was talking about. About Bree's injury, Shea's dazzling play, and the girl who inspired the fans to cheer.

Today's instruction was to befriend Bree. Lily and Madison had talked about it on the way to school. And they had prayed about it—for wisdom and courage for Lily to say and do the right thing. Lily was ready. At least she hoped so.

The next step was to find Bree.

It wasn't hard.

The girl hobbled down the hall on crutches, surrounded by supportive teammates and fans. Lily watched Bree's entourage peel away one by one until it was just Bree at her locker.

Lily took a slow breath as she approached the injured athlete. "Hi Bree. I wanted to see if there's anything I could do to help?" Lily lifted her pitch at the end to turn her statement into a question.

Hunched over and leaning on her crutches, Bree twisted her head sideways to peer up at Lily. She straightened her frame and glared. "Can you make it so I can play? Of course not. So there's nothing you can do to help."

"Does it hurt?"

"That's a stupid question." Bree huffed. "Only when I try to walk. Other than that, everything is just peachy."

"Sorry. I didn't mean to upset you."

Bree blew out air as she closed her eyes. When she opened them, they emanated sorrow. "I'm sorry. I shouldn't be mad at you. It's just that after I went down, the next thing I heard was you cheering my replacement. It stung."

"I just wanted to encourage Shea," Lily said. "It was the first time she got to play all season."

"So right. Shea played brilliantly and scored the winning basket, but it was your cheering that made it happen. And that win qualified us for the playoffs. So it's all good for her, the team, and the school. It just sucks for me."

"But it was your great playing all season long that brought us to this point," Lily said. "Don't forget that."

"Yes, but I'll end up watching them on their playoff run. And I'll miss my last remaining hope of landing a basketball scholarship."

"Or you could shift your role. Instead of leading from the floor, lead from the bench." Lily studied Bree to see if it clicked. "Like I told Shea, don't be a benchwarmer. Be a difference-maker."

"I'm not sure I know how to do that."

Lily tipped her head to peer at Bree. "Do you ever pray?"

"Uh, yeah. I guess. Once in a while."

"I'm just beginning to learn how," Lily said. "Can I pray for you?"

Bree shrugged. "Couldn't hurt."

Lily held out her palm toward Bree. "Lord, please encourage Bree. Show her how to be a difference-maker for her team, how to encourage them to do their very best. In Jesus's name, amen."

Bree's eyes brimmed with appreciation. "I don't think anyone's ever prayed for me before, at least not like that." She smiled. "I feel better. Thanks."

"You're welcome. Now, about your ankle?"

Bree shrugged. "What about it? I'm out for the season."

"In the Bible, Jesus healed people. So did his followers."

"So you think you're like Jesus?"

"No way, but the Bible says we're supposed to heal people in Jesus's name. I'm just learning about that."

"How many people have you healed so far?"

"You'll be my first."

"That's gutsy . . . and a little weird too, but a good kind of weird."

Lily sucked in a slow breath, bolstering her confidence. She bent down, hovering her hand at the side of Bree's ankle. "Jesus, I command Bree's ankle to be healed. Take away the pain. Thanks." Lily straightened up and looked at Bree.

"Now what?" Bree asked.

"Good question." Lily thought about it. "I guess

you're healed." She cocked her head to the side. "Does your ankle feel any different?"

"Maybe. Possibly." Bree put a bit of weight on it to test it. "It doesn't hurt as much. I think it might be a bit better."

"You can receive healing in faith," Lily said, "or let doubt take it away."

"You're certainly a strange one, Lily Thatcher."

"That's how I roll."

14

BIBLE STUDY

Lily had to wait until lunch to update Madison on what had happened with her and Bree. It was probably her most successful task yet. It was all because she and Madison had prayed about it. And discussing what to do helped too.

Madison's self-determined meal chart—which Lily had embraced as her own—called for hamburgers on Monday. As the girls waited in the short line for their burgers, Lily turned to Madison. "Thanks for buying my lunch every day. But once I get my first paycheck, I want to start paying for my food."

"Did your book tell you to do that?"

Lily shook her head. "It wasn't in my book, but

it wasn't really my idea either. Can God put ideas into our heads?"

"The Holy Spirit can speak to us," Madison said. "All we need to do is listen."

"I expected you to say, 'Listen and obey,' but you didn't."

"I don't need to," Madison said. "You already know that. We listen to God and then do what he says. It's that simple."

After getting their food, they sat at a table by themselves at the edge of the cafeteria. Madison thanked God for their meals and bit into her burger. Lily didn't. She unshouldered her backpack and pulled out her notebook. She opened it to the latest entry and read it to Madison. "It says, 'Ask Madison to do a Bible study with you.' But I don't get it. What's that mean?"

Madison wrinkled her nose. "Ah, we do a Bible study."

"Yeah, but what does it mean? I understand *Bible*, and I understand *study*. But putting them together confuses me. Is it a class we take at church? Do we need a textbook? Is there an app we need or a website to follow? Do we need to find a teacher?"

"Sorry," Madison said. "It makes sense to me. I never thought it might be confusing to you. A Bible study is quite simple. We read a passage, and then we talk about it."

"So you explain it to me?"

"No. We explain it to each other."

"Yeah, like I'll ever be able to explain anything about the Bible to you."

"But you already have," Madison confirmed. "You look at the Bible with fresh eyes and catch things I've overlooked for years. We sharpen each other, like iron sharpening iron."

Lily thought about that a moment. "Iron sharpening iron?"

"Also in the Bible." Madison grinned.

"Okay. I guess that makes sense. But what happens when we get to a passage you don't understand? You know a lot and all, but what do we do then?"

"No one knows everything about the Bible. When we get to something we don't understand, we talk about it. We pray about it. We ask God for help. Sometimes it happens right away, but not always."

"When should we do it?" Lily asked. "With school and work and everything else, I don't know where we can ever fit it in."

"We shouldn't try to fit it in. Instead, we make it

a priority and fit other things around it. Just like reading the Bible each day, we should study it each day too."

"But you read your Bible in the morning, and I read it last thing before I go to sleep. They don't align. Your best time is my worst, and my best time isn't good for you."

Madison chewed thoughtfully and stroked her chin. "What if we did a Bible study here in the cafeteria during lunch?"

"Is that even allowed?"

"Of course it is. We'll be doing it during our free time, no teachers will be involved, and it won't use any school materials. It's a perfect solution."

"But what if other people see us?" Lily asked. "Or want to join?"

"That'd be cool!" Madison said. "The more the merrier. And if we fill up one table, we'll just start another group. I'm really liking this idea. So cool."

"Should we start tomorrow," Lily asked, "with Genesis chapter one, verse one?"

"We could," Madison said. "But let's start with one of the gospels."

"What's a gospel?" Lily asked. "I've heard the minister use that word, but I don't know what it means."

"Remember when I told you the Bible has four biographies of Jesus?"

Lily nodded.

Madison continued. "Matthew, Mark, Luke, and John. We call them gospels because they tell us the good news about Jesus."

"I've been reading from Luke each night, just like you told me," Lily said. "Should we study that?"

"We could. Or maybe John. John's writing is almost like poetry, which makes it great for a discussion. You pick."

"I've already read through Luke a couple times," Lily said. "Let's do John."

"It's settled," Madison said. "We'll start John tomorrow."

That's when Jason strolled over with his tray of food. He plopped onto a seat across from them. "Sup, guys?" He chomped into his pizza.

Lily glanced at Madison, who scowled at her recently confirmed boyfriend. "Dude, try again."

Jason frowned at her, and then a gleam formed. "I bid you a fond good day, dear maidens. May I perchance join you for our noontime sustenance?"

"You've been reading too much Shakespeare,"

Madison said. "Try for the middle ground, something fitting for your girlfriend."

Jason smirked. "I can't very well kiss you in front of the kid." He tipped his head toward Lily. That's when he noticed her open book. "What's that?"

Lily felt her face warm. Surely she was blushing. Based on the intensity of the heat, she assumed she was bright red. "It's nothing." She slammed the book shut. "It's personal." She shoved it into her backpack and zipped the compartment shut.

Jason held up his hands. "Oops. Must have touched a nerve. Sorry."

"We were just talking about doing a Bible study here at school during lunch," Madison explained.

"Cool!" Jason said. "May I join?"

Now it was Madison's turn to smirk. "Only if you're not a total tool about it."

15

FORGIVE

After school, Lily waited for Madison at her car.

Madison strolled up, genial as usual. Perhaps even more so. "You must have had quite a day. First is everyone affirming you for cheering at the game. Then your interaction with Bree. And now our plans to begin Bible study."

"I checked my notebook," Lily said as Madison drove home. "It said, 'Well done! Studying the Bible during lunch is an excellent idea.' So it looks like we're good there."

"But you don't look so happy."

"There are two more tasks. I need a break. How come I get more stuff to do than you did when you had the book?"

"I got a lot of them too," Madison said. "It's just that I didn't share all of them with you."

"Why not?"

"Some were easy, and I didn't need help." Madison paused. "And some of them were about you."

"Like what?"

"One was to invite you to church. If I'd told you beforehand, you would have felt pressured into going. I didn't want that."

Lily gave a slow nod. "Makes sense. What else?"

"Several of them told me to be prepared to talk about certain topics with you. Like mercy, grace, salvation, and . . ."

"And what?"

"Forgiveness."

"Seriously? Is that why you wanted me to forgive my mom?"

Madison nodded.

"You're not going to believe it," Lily said. "One of my new instructions is to forgive her. But I'm not going to. I told God so. No way. No how. And I won't visit her in jail either. Never, ever."

Madison drew a deep breath. A glimmer of frustration flashed across her face and then vanished just as fast. "Does your mom know you're upset with her?"

Lily had to think about it. "Guess not."

"Then not forgiving her isn't hurting her at all, but it's eating at you. I think we forgive other people for our benefit just as much as theirs."

"But she's done so much stuff to me. Why do I have to forgive her? I don't suppose the Bible says to?"

"It does," Madison said. "One line in the Lord's Prayer asks God to forgive us just as we forgive others. If we withhold forgiveness from them, we're giving him permission to withhold it from us."

This confused Lily. "I guess that's one way to look at it."

"To make it perfectly clear, right after this, Matthew writes that Jesus says if we forgive others, God will forgive us. But if we don't forgive others, God won't forgive us."

"I'm confused. I thought that when we follow Jesus, all our sins, both past and present, are forgiven. Is that wrong?"

"Jesus talks about this in a parable," Madison said. "He says—"

"Wait a sec," Lily interrupted. "What's a parable?"

"It's a simple story that reveals spiritual truth."

"Got it," Lily said. "What's the story?"

"There was a man who owed his master a lot of money, more than he could ever repay. When the master went to throw the servant in jail for his great debt, the man begged for mercy, and the master gave it to him. But then the man went to someone else who owed him a little. This man also begged for mercy, but the servant refused and threw the guy in jail. When the master heard about it, he reinstated the wicked servant's original punishment."

"Wow!" Lily said. "That servant sure didn't get it. How could he be so stupid?"

"Jesus says that God will do the same for us if we withhold forgiveness."

"Wait. You mean I'm like the servant?"

"God forgave you of everything, so you need to do the same for your mom."

"But she doesn't deserve to be forgiven."

Madison glanced at Lily and gave a comforting gaze. "And neither did you—or me. But God did it anyway."

"But the parable is about forgiveness versus judgment," Lily sputtered. "What about grace and mercy?"

"We have to balance God's grace and mercy

with his justice," Madison said. "It's hard for me to grasp, knowing that I'm forgiven of everything, but that there might be an exception." Madison furled her eyebrows and then lit up. "But if we forgive everyone of everything, then it isn't an issue."

"Got it. Now it makes sense why you wanted me to forgive my mom and why my book told me to do it. But how can I forgive her?" Lily scrunched her eyebrows. "Especially when I don't want to."

"It starts with prayer," Madison said.

Lily groaned. "It seems everything does."

"First, ask God to change your heart toward your mother. Then pray that God will bless her."

"What if I don't want to?"

"Do it anyway," Madison said. "Jesus tells us to love our enemies and pray for them. Though your mom's not quite like an enemy, it still fits."

Lily leaned back in her seat and closed her eyes. It was hard to take in. It was even harder to do. She slowly exhaled and then inhaled even more deliberately, supernatural courage building inside her as she did. She opened her eyes and peered at Madison. "How about you pray for me? And my mom?"

"I'll start," Madison said. "You finish."

16

AUTHORITY

Lily ended her prayer and opened her eyes. Full of concern, she turned to look at Madison, who continued driving home. Lily studied her best friend's face, seeking a reaction. She got none. "I think I said the right words, but I didn't mean them. Is that a sin?"

Madison's lips curled up just a tad. "I see it as obedience. Each time you pray for your mom you'll mean it a little bit more. Before long, it'll be genuine."

Lily groaned. "I have to keep doing it?"

"I think so," Madison said. "Here's an idea. Every time you think of your mom, pray for her."

"Every time?"

"Yep."

"Then I won't think about her."

Understanding covered Madison's face. "Good luck with that. If you try not to think about her, you'll think about her even more . . . which will give you more opportunities to pray."

"Are you speaking from experience?"

Madison grinned. "Don't fight it. The best way forward is to embrace it."

Lily considered Madison's advice. It sounded wise, but she still didn't like it. She needed to think about this, to really contemplate it. At last she spoke. "My other instruction was even more confusing."

"What is it?" Madison asked.

"Be respectful to the policeman and answer his questions."

"Sounds simple enough."

"Not for me. Mom taught me to always avoid the cops, to hide or run, and to refuse to answer any questions."

"My parents taught me the opposite," Madison said. "As long as we're not doing anything wrong, we have no reason to be afraid."

"What if the cops are corrupt?" Lily asked.

"God says to respect authority. He put them in

place for our benefit. So I choose to trust him with that."

Lily was still thinking about authority as she read her Bible that evening. She came across a verse in Luke that mentioned it, but it didn't apply to her situation. So she did a word search for *authority*. After looking at several passages, she found Romans 13:1–5, which seemed to be exactly what Madison had told her.

Lily read the passage over and over, sometimes slowly and at other times fast. It was difficult to accept. She understood the command easily enough. That was straightforward. But trusting it enough to change her own thinking was hard. It confronted everything her mother had taught her about dealing with authority, especially the police. It was just one more item on the long list of things she held against her mother, which again brought up the need to forgive her—and to pray for her.

Yuck! Lily winced. *Being a Christian is hard. Who would've thought?*

Struggling to make sense of the passage about authority, she asked God to help her understand. She was still working on it when her eyelids grew heavy. She allowed them to flutter closed for just a second. The next thing she knew it was morning. Her open Bible lay next to her on the bed.

Lily talked with Madison about the passage on the way to school and again at lunch. Though they opened their Bibles, they never got to John.

This bothered Lily, but not Madison. "It still counts, even if it wasn't what we planned to discuss."

Lily was still thinking about respecting authority when she was called to the principal's office after lunch. Principal Gardner was a good man. He'd always been kind to her and sympathetic to her home situation. She'd never thought about it until now, but he'd always offered her grace. Lily trusted him, making it easy to accept his authority. It was a good first step toward doing what the Bible said to do.

Or maybe not.

When she arrived, Principal Gardner was pleasant enough, but something felt off. His face was pale, and his eyes looked sad. He beckoned her to enter his office. She did.

A harsh-looking police officer waited. His young frame stood at rigid attention, shoulders back, head held high, and hands clasped behind his back. Fear rose within her, and she fought an impulse to flee.

All thoughts of respecting authority vanished. The voice of Lily's mom reverberated in her head. "Never trust the cops. They're just out to get you. Don't tell them a thing." Lily set her jaw and glared up at the uniformed man.

"I'm here to take you in for questioning," he said.

Lily leaned forward and rose on her toes, making herself look a little taller and a lot more hostile. She glared up at him. "No."

"You don't have a choice."

"But I do. You can't haul me in without charges."

Principal Gardner edged toward the officer. He held up his hand. "This isn't what we agreed to and is getting out of control. Let's take a moment and calm down."

The policeman glared at Gardner. "I can arrest you for interfering with an official investigation. Do you want me to do that?"

"That won't be necessary," Principal Gardner said. "But please treat her with respect and dignity. She isn't a threat."

"That's not how I see it," the officer shot back.

"She's a good student and a good person. But

you're frightening her unnecessarily. Given your demeanor, her response is understandable."

The officer slowly shook his head and turned back to Lily. "Are you refusing?"

"Yes!"

"Then I'll restrain you." The officer extended an arm toward her.

Principal Gardner stepped between them. "Easy now. Let's all just calm down," he said to the policeman. Then he shifted his stern look to Lily, confirming that he meant her too.

"As a courtesy," Principal Gardner said to the officer, "I extended hospitality to you when you arrived, but now I must insist you leave."

Without blinking, the officer stared at the principal. Gardner narrowed his gaze and glared back.

The officer blinked first. "Fine." He huffed and stomped out of the principal's office.

17

BE RESPECTFUL

Principal Gardner watched the officer leave and then turned to face Lily. "I should have stopped this sooner. I'm sorry."

The verse about authority surged back into Lily's mind. "No worries. You've always done what's right for me. I trust you."

Principal Gardner gestured toward the chair in front of his desk. "Why don't you have a seat and take a few minutes to collect yourself. I'll get you some water."

"Thanks, but I'm good."

"Are you sure?"

"Yep. Good to go."

But am I?

As Lily shuffled to her locker, she replayed what

had happened. She had respected Principal Gardener's authority, but not the officer's. He'd only asked her one question, and she'd answered—even if it wasn't the answer he wanted. Had she obeyed the notebook's instruction? Technically she had, but it didn't sit right with her.

Someone tapped her on her shoulder. It was Hannah. "Lily, there's a policeman in the parking lot. He says he has one more question for you."

Lily turned and followed Hannah outside, who pointed to her left.

"Thanks," Lily said. Now she'd have a second chance to do what the book said and answer his questions.

She tried to smile, something she'd never done before to the police. It was hard, but she pulled it off—sort of.

"Will you let me escort you to the station?" the officer asked.

"No!" Lily wouldn't go without a fight. "What are the charges?"

The young officer's face went blank. He glanced to his right. "Ahh, for receiving stolen property, conspiring to commit fraud, and . . . for murder." He approached the shocked Lily, grabbed her shoulder, and spun her around. Before Lily knew what was happening, the officer had cuffed both her hands behind her back. He ratcheted the restraints tight.

She winced.

The officer grabbed Lily's upper arm and shoved her toward his car. "Please don't make this any more difficult than it already is."

Shocked students gawked as the policeman pulled her toward his patrol car. Everything she had learned about respecting authority over the past few days was quickly replaced with everything her mom had taught her over the past eighteen years.

Lily even called him a name, but she stopped short of spitting on him, something she'd seen her mother do too often. That had never worked out well for her mom, so why should she do it?

He opened the rear door of the patrol car and gave her a bit of a shove when she didn't move fast enough for him. As she fell into the backseat, her head smacked the doorframe. The door slammed shut, and the lock clicked. He sped away with lights flashing and siren blaring.

That's when Lily thought to pray, something she should've done sooner, much sooner. "God, this is a nightmare. Get me through this. Show me how to be respectful as the Bible teaches. Give me strength. Please."

Still sprawled across the backseat of the squad car, an ethereal peace flowed into Lily. Her tense body relaxed, and her raging emotions subsided. She remembered the story of Paul and Silas being arrested. In jail they prayed and sang hymns. Then a miracle happened, and they were free. *If only I knew some church songs well enough to sing them. But at least I can pray.*

She did. Clarity emerged. With effort she righted herself. Gathering her resolve, she looked at the officer in his rearview mirror. "I'm sorry for giving you a hassle."

The policeman glanced at her in the mirror but didn't say a thing. He did, however, slow his driving. He jabbed a couple of buttons on his console. The lights stopped flashing, and the siren fell silent.

When they arrived at the station, he helped her out of the police car. This time he wasn't as rough. Almost gentle. He escorted her into the building and left her in an interrogation room. He pulled the door shut with a click.

If only he would've uncuffed me.

But Lily chose not to think about how much her wrists hurt and her arms ached. Instead, she prayed. As she did, she felt God filling her with resolve to do exactly what the passage said to do about respecting authority—no matter how difficult it would be. She even prayed for the officer.

Soon Lily heard a combative conversation outside the door. The voices grew louder and more heated. "This isn't at all what you were supposed to do," someone said.

Then came some groveling from the officer who had hauled her in.

"I'll deal with you later," the first voice said.

Then the door opened. "Lily, I'm so sorry for what just happened."

The man looked familiar, she thought maybe from church.

"I apologize on behalf of the entire police force. Let me get those cuffs off you."

As Lily rubbed her sore wrists, the man extended his hand to her. "I'm Detective Brindle. But you can call me Don."

Lily shook his hand as she recalled the words *respect authority*. "It's nice to meet you. Thank you for removing the handcuffs."

"That should never have happened," Don said. "I'm so sorry. Let's get out of here and go somewhere more comfortable." With gentle care, Don ushered Lily down the hall, up some stairs, and around a corner, emerging into an inviting lounge. A large window overlooked a picturesque pond behind the building. Don moved a chair in front of the window and offered it to Lily. Then he pulled one up for himself. They both sat. "This is much better," Don said.

Lily recalled the instruction in her book: to be respectful to the police. "If I may ask, sir, why was I arrested?"

"Arrested? You weren't arrested. The officer confirmed that with me."

Lily replayed the scene in her mind. The man had never said he was arresting her or stated her rights. "Then why the handcuffs?"

"He made a grave error in judgment," Don said. "He was supposed to *ask* you if you were willing to come in to answer a few questions and then give you a ride if you agreed."

"He gave me a ride, all right." Lily massaged her wrists. "The officer said something about theft, conspiracy, and murder."

"Those are some of the charges facing your mother."

"Murder?"

"Your former landlord died as a result of his altercation with your mother."

Remorse filled Lily. Though she had never liked the man, he was nice enough—at least for a slum landlord. But now he was dead. His life was over. She wondered if he knew Jesus. She feared not. For him, it was too late.

Then Lily thought of her mom sitting in jail for murder. She suddenly wished she had visited when Madison had first suggested it. Lily also knew she was one step closer to being able to forgive her mom. *Help me, Lord,* she prayed silently. *Show me how to forgive her as you forgave me.*

18

ANSWERING QUESTIONS

"I want to ask you about a Buddha statue," Detective Brindle said. "Did your mom have one?"

Lily fought off her lifelong training to be evasive. She knew she needed to answer his questions truthfully, but it took her a moment to corral her thoughts. "It showed up a couple of months ago. I'm not sure where she got it, and she wouldn't say, but I felt icky around it."

"Do you know where it is now?"

Lily scoured her memory, trying to recall if she had seen the Buddha statue sitting in front of the apartment building after their eviction. She couldn't. "I don't, but Madison might. Aside from my clothes and a few personal things, Madison sold everything she could, and neighbors carried away the rest. Why do you need to know?"

"A certain individual has accused her of stealing it from him, and he wants it back. He's most adamant. We suspect it may contain contraband."

"I could text Madison once school gets out," Lily said, "but my phone's in my backpack, which is still at school."

Don Brindle pulled out his phone and handed it to Lily. "Use mine."

Lily shrugged. "I don't know her number. All I know is that it's three digits higher than Dad's, but that doesn't help much."

"That helps a lot," Don said. "I have his number." Then he explained. "Mark and I often volunteer together at church." He punched several buttons, swiped a couple times, and handed it to her. It was ringing.

Soon Madison answered. "Mr. Brindle?"

"No, it's Lily. I'm just using his phone."

"Where in the world are you?" Madison asked. "I've been worried sick."

"I'm at the police station," Lily said.

"So am I."

"Where?" Lily asked. "Are you skipping school?"

"Principal Gardner gave me permission to leave." Then Madison answered Lily's first question. "I think I'm at the front desk in the main lobby."

The detective motioned for his phone.

"Mr. Brindle wants to talk to you," Lily told Madison. Then she passed it to him.

"Hi, Madison. Will you hand your phone to the desk clerk? Tell him Detective Brindle wants to talk." Don waited. "Please have someone accompany the young lady to the upper observation lounge. It's urgent . . . Thank you."

In no time, a police officer brought Madison to the lounge. A puffy-eyed Madison rushed forward and wrapped her arms around Lily. "Don't worry, it's going to be okay. Dad's on his way."

"That won't be necessary," Don said. "It was all just a tremendous misunderstanding."

Lily nodded to Madison.

"But I heard you got arrested for murder," Madison said.

"I sent a rookie officer to do a simple job, but he made a series of poor decisions," Don said. "I suspect his first week on the force will also be his last."

Madison cast a questioning glance at Lily. "So you're okay?"

"Yes," Lily said. "Mr. Brindle just had some questions."

Don nodded. "Let me call Mark and explain the situation."

As he stepped away, Lily turned back to Madison. "Thank you for coming to rescue me."

"But you didn't need me after all," Madison said.

"That's where you're wrong," Lily replied. "Do you remember a Buddha statue when we were evicted?"

"I do," Madison said. "I felt it was evil and stayed away from it."

"Did you sell it?"

"No. I gave it away. I think to one of your neighbors."

"Do you remember who?"

"A boy begged his mom for it, and I let them take it."

Don heard this as he returned. "What did they look like?"

"The boy was probably around eight. Pudgy

with a mohawk haircut. The mom had pink, spiked hair, a snake tattoo on her left arm, and her right eyebrow was pierced—in three places."

"That's most detailed," the detective said.

"They were easy to remember," Madison replied.

"I don't know their names," Lily added, "but they live in 3D."

"That's exactly the information I need," Don said. "That wraps up our first order of business."

"There's more?" Lily asked.

Don nodded. "I also want to talk to you about the theft of your identity."

"Can you fix it?" Lily asked.

"I'm not sure. Maybe, but it will take time and hinge on how cooperative your mother wants to be."

Lily's hope for a simple resolution faded.

"It might just be simpler to change your name and start over." Don chuckled.

Lily wasn't sure if he was serious or not.

"But to conduct a formal investigation," Don said, "I need you to first file a complaint."

"I don't want my mom to get into any more trouble than she's already in."

"That's most admirable of you, but it's a path

you must go down if you have any hope of restoring your credit . . . and avoiding any future confusion."

"Confusion?" Lily asked.

"It seems your mom has been using your name for a lot of things," Don explained. "That likely led to the confusion the officer had when he came to get you. He knew all that your mom was accused of, which had your name connected to it. It's possible he thought he was dealing with a suspected murderer."

"Okay, then," Lily said. "Let's do it." She answered all his questions as he typed into his laptop.

Don scanned the information. "That covers it."

"Thank you." Lily stood to leave.

"One last thing," Don said, "is to fill out a complaint about the officer. I presume you want to do that."

Lily thought about how badly the guy had treated her, the bump on her head, and her chafed wrists. But she wanted to take a different path, a God-honoring one. She shook her head. "Let's skip it. I choose mercy. I want to forgive him."

19

OBEDIENCE AT LAST

The girls walked to Madison's car and got in. Madison went to start it, but Lily reached out her hand to stop her. "I think I'm ready."

"Ready for what?" Madison turned to face Lily.

"To forgive my mom." Lily dipped her head once to confirm. "Yes, I'm ready. How do I do it?"

"What do you mean?" Madison asked.

"Is there a special prayer I'm supposed to say? Or a Bible passage to read? Or maybe a thing I'm supposed to do at church . . . like a ritual or a ceremony?"

"It's more just something you do in your heart," Madison said. "Since your mom doesn't know you're mad at her, this is mostly between you and God."

"I feel like I need to at least pray," Lily said.

Madison nodded. "Good idea."

"Okay then. Ahh, God, I forgive my mom for all that she's done to me and the mistakes she made in raising me. Help me to really mean this and not take it back. Okay, then. Amen."

"Good job," Madison said. "How do you feel?"

"Well . . . I feel better. That's for sure," Lily said. She thought about it some more. "Relieved. Free. Like a mega weight has been lifted from me. And I'm sort of happy."

"You're probably feeling joy. Forgiving someone can do that."

"Yes, it must be joy. That's it! I feel joy. It's something I'm not used to." Lily grinned. "And I like it."

"That's wonderful," Madison said.

"Why didn't I do it sooner? You should've made me."

Madison gave a wry smile and slowly shook her head. "It had to be a decision you made, and you couldn't make it until you were ready. But I'm glad you did. Now you can move on."

"Instead of hating my mom," Lily said, "I now

feel sorry for her. She's had a rough life, and it's not going to get any better. I think I'm finally ready to visit her in jail."

Madison checked the time. "Should we go now?"

"But I don't know where she's being held or what the visiting hours are. Maybe I can find out, and we can go Saturday after work."

"Or we can go today," Madison said. "I already checked and know where she is. We can visit now."

Lily blinked back her emotions. "You're a good friend. The best ever."

Thirty-five minutes later, a prison guard ushered Lily into the visiting area of the prison. There was no one there. Lily scanned the room and picked a table in the corner that she thought her mom would be most comfortable at. She sat and waited. And waited. At last another door opened, and a guard escorted in Lily's mom.

Her mother paused when she saw Lily, and her haggard face lit up. She almost smiled. Lily couldn't remember the last time she'd seen her mom happy. Lily stood and gestured to the empty chair on the other side of the table. Her mother moved toward it, slowly at first and then with more purpose.

Lily felt an impulse to give her mom a hug, something she never remembered doing, but the guard had warned her to avoid physical contact. When her mother reached the chair, the two women stood there staring at each other. No one said a word. At last Lily sat. So did her mom.

"Thanks for coming to see me." Lily's mother blinked twice and then grimaced. "After all I've done to you, I wasn't expecting to ever see you again, but I'm sure glad you came."

"It took me a while to get to that point," Lily said, "but God has been working in my life. He helped me forgive you."

"God?" Lily's mom snorted. "Did you get religion or something?"

"You might say that. I decided to follow Jesus."

"Well, it must be working out for you." Lily's mom scanned her. "You look different. Content. At peace. You also look healthy. Where have you been staying? At the women's shelter?"

"I made a friend at school and moved in with her. Her name is Madison."

"Are you her project or something?"

"More like a best friend and sister all rolled into

one. Her parents treat me like family. And her brother, well, her brother is someone special." Lily tried not to let her face reveal just how much she thought of Michael, but her glow burst forth anyway.

"I guess I should be happy for you then," Lily's mom said. "It looks like you're getting the break I never had." Then she hung her head.

"Mom, why did you steal my identity? You ruined my credit, and I almost got arrested—for things that you did."

Her mother let out a slow sigh. "Sorry."

"I had to fill out a complaint to try to fix it. Detective Brindle will probably talk to you about it. Will you cooperate with him? For my sake?"

Her mother shrugged. "I guess it wouldn't hurt."

"It might even help," Lily said. "You know, if you cooperate."

Lily's mom gave a thoughtful nod. "I really made a mess of things, Lils."

For as long as Lily could remember, her mom had always called her Lils. Though she never liked that nickname, it wasn't until this exact moment that she realized just how much she had missed hearing it.

Lily reached out her hand and laid it on her mom's. She glanced at the guard from the corner of her eye. He didn't react. "Though there's not much I can do, I can pray for you. I'll pray for you every day and ask God to be with you. And I'll pray that you give your life to Jesus."

Lily's mom snorted. "I doubt anyone's ever prayed for me before. But don't think you can convert me or something. God has ignored me my whole life, so I'm going to ignore him for the rest of mine. Seems fitting."

"But that won't stop me from praying for you. Count on it."

"I appreciate that," Lily's mom said, "even if I don't think it will do any good."

Lily stood. "Would you like me to visit you again, Mom?"

"That would be nice, Lils. I'd really like that." For the first time in a long time, her mother smiled.

20

FOUR MORE

The first thing Lily did when she arrived at school the next morning was head straight to the principal's office to retrieve her backpack.

"I apologize, Lily," Principal Gardner told her. "In retrospect, I could have handled things differently."

"No problem," Lily said. "Everything worked out. It was all a huge misunderstanding."

"I know," the principal replied. "I talked with the police commissioner, and she told me that what happened should never have occurred. She also promised me it would never happen again. Then I informed the entire student body and staff, assuring them you had done nothing wrong."

"Thank you, sir," Lily said, pleased at how easily she was picking up Madison's respectful manners.

It wasn't until toward the end of second-period English that Lily had a chance to peek in her notebook. The first new entry delighted her. "I am pleased with your obedience, Lils. You forgave your mother and visited her in prison. Well done, good and faithful servant."

Satisfaction flooded into Lily's soul, and her heart melted at God using her nickname. *He so gets me.*

Then she turned the page. She groaned silently. In just a few hours, God had given her four new instructions. *How many came in last night, and how many were from today?*

The first message said, "Tell Madison that Mom is mentoring you. Don't hide it from her."

The next page said, "Talk to Jason's mom about his dad." This confused Lily even more. *Who am I to interfere? What can I tell her, anyway?*

Then came, "Pay rent, like Madison." Lily

relaxed. The Monroes required their children to pay a token rent once they had their first job. It was to teach them how to handle money. Lily was already planning on doing that as soon as she got her first paycheck. It would also show she saw them as her family. *I got this!*

The fourth page said, "Look into adult adoption." Lily had never heard of such a thing, but she was curious. She'd do it as soon as school was out and she could use her phone.

She planned to share her new instructions with Madison at lunch, before they began their Bible study. But that didn't work out.

Jason joined them today. Lily didn't think he knew about her notebook, and she didn't want to have to try to explain it to him. But they did have an amazing discussion on the beginning of John chapter one.

Lily had to wait until after school to talk to Madison about the four new entries. She was nervous about the first one. It took a couple of minutes into their drive home for Lily to muster enough courage to ask. "My book told me to ask Mom to mentor me, but is that okay with you?"

"Of course it is," Madison said. "Why wouldn't it be?"

"She's your mom. I don't want you to think I'm trying to come between you two."

"It's all good," Madison answered. "You're family. We're like sisters. As far as I'm concerned, my mom and dad are your mom and dad."

"I just wanted to double-check." Lily paused. "We've been doing it for a while."

"I know," Madison said. "But thanks for telling me."

This news shocked Lily, but she kept her surprise to herself. "And there's another thing."

"What's that?"

"I'm also confused by a second instruction. It says to 'talk to Jason's mom about his dad.' But she doesn't know me, and I have nothing to say."

"Interesting," Madison said. "I've felt God telling me the same thing. Let's pray about it. Maybe we can do it together."

Lily agreed. It would certainly be easier for the two of them to meet Jason's mom together, but Lily still wasn't sure what she could say or how she could help. It still felt like interference. Preoccupied with this, Lily didn't bring up the last two instructions. Instead, she prayed about this one.

Soon after they got home, Madison received a text asking her to come into work. Just her. Not Lily.

Their boss only needed one, and since Lily couldn't drive, that meant Madison.

Madison started to apologize, but Lily stopped her.

"It's just as well," Lily said. "I've got a ton of homework to catch up on from yesterday."

Madison dashed off to work, and Lily went to the kitchen to help Mom prepare supper. "Mom, I really appreciate you mentoring me."

"It's my pleasure and a true joy," Mom said.

"You're really helping me better understand spiritual stuff," Lily said. "Dad too. Also Michael. Especially Madison. But . . ."

"But what?"

"I need your help in becoming an adult. The right way. The godly way. And to . . ."

"And to what?" Mom asked.

Lily felt her face grow warm. She considered what she would say and at last found the right words. "Well, someday, maybe . . . to be a good wife and mom . . . just like you. My mother did everything wrong, and I want to do everything right."

"Don't put me on a pedestal," Mom said. "I'm far from perfect, but with God's help I'll do all I can to prepare you to be a God-honoring woman, wife, and mother."

"God-honoring." Lily smiled at the term. "I like that."

"Let me pray for you before we do anything else." Mom extended her right hand and placed it on Lily's head. She proclaimed a blessing on Lily to become a God-honoring woman, preparing her for marriage and motherhood when the time came.

Lily opened her eyes. "Thank you!" She gave Mom an appreciative glance. "Since it's Madison's turn to clean up after the meal, I'll cover for her. Maybe after that we can talk some more."

"Or we can both clean up and talk as we work."

"Perfect."

21

WRONG ASSUMPTIONS

"Mom mentoring me is going really great," Lily told Madison on their drive to school. "Last night we talked about Queen Esther and how she risked her life to do the right thing. So inspiring. And we'll go grocery shopping together and do meal planning."

"I'm sure Mom will like that." A gleam formed on Madison's face. "As a bonus, it'll get me off the hook of going with her. I so don't like grocery shopping."

"Her mentoring me is the good part," Lily said. "Now the bad."

"What?"

"I thought I was getting the hang of obeying God's instructions," Lily said. "But now I have to break up with Michael. I don't want to do that. I really, really, really don't."

"Break up with Michael? Are you sure? It just doesn't feel right."

"Yup." Lily thought about it. "Do you think I can talk God out of it?"

"Maybe you're misunderstanding his instruction," Madison suggested.

"Nope."

"Read it to me, exactly what your book says."

"Okay." Lily pulled the notebook from her backpack and opened it. "It says, 'Let him down easy; be kind.' But I don't want to."

"You know that for my first instruction I went on a date with Ryan," Madison said, "but I never told you the details. My book said, 'When he asks you to the movies, don't hesitate. Say yes.' I assumed it meant Jason, but I was wrong."

"So you expected Jason to ask you out, and he didn't. But Ryan did."

"Correct," Madison said. "You assume your book means Michael. But it just says *he*. That could be anybody—half the population, in fact. And I doubt it's Michael. I seriously doubt it."

"But who could it be?" Lily asked. "The guys at

school don't know I exist, and the guys at work ignore me."

"I don't know," Madison said. "Just be ready to obey God when the time comes."

Lily agreed and then spent the rest of the day praying that it wasn't Michael.

It still weighed on her as the girls walked to the parking lot after school.

"There's some dude standing next to my car," Madison hissed. "He has a bouquet of flowers."

The guy stood at rigid attention, shoulders back and head held high. His right hand gripped the blooms, with his left hand behind his back.

"He looks familiar," Lily whispered. "I think it's the guy who hauled me in yesterday, but he looks different without his uniform. Younger."

"Dude looks like he's in college," Madison said. "Probably Michael's age, if that."

"Michael's more handsome. A lot more."

The girls slowed their pace as they approached the grinning guy. They also edged closer to each other, with their arms brushing.

The guy took one step forward. "Hi," he said to Lily. "I'm Ian." His smile broadened, showing off a perfect row of bright white teeth. He extended his arm toward her. "These are for you."

With caution, Lily approached him and accepted the flowers. "Thank you. They're lovely," she said without even bothering to look. Then she stepped back to stand next to Madison. Her body shaking, Lily pushed her shoulder into Madison's upper arm for comfort—and support.

"Thank you for not filing a complaint against me yesterday," the guy said. "Though I deserved it, I really appreciate that you didn't." He brought his right arm behind his back to join his left. "They suspended me without pay. There will be a hearing, and my brief career in law enforcement is probably over." His white teeth disappeared from view and then reappeared just as quickly. "I thought that to properly thank you for not making it any worse, I could take you out for dinner sometime."

"You mean like a date?"

Ian looked away. "Oh, no." He fidgeted. "Not a date." He returned his gaze. "Well, not really." He shifted his weight from one foot to the other. "Not unless you'd like it to be a date."

The idea horrified Lily.

Even though she had forgiven him and chose to offer him mercy by not filing a complaint, that didn't mean she had any feelings for him. None whatsoever. Nada.

As she got ready to let him have it and tell him exactly what she thought of his terrible idea, she remembered her notebook's instruction. *Let him down easy. Be kind.* Okay, she could do that.

Lily took a half step toward him, grateful to feel Madison's hand rest on her shoulder blade as she did. *Madison's got my back.*

Now filled with confidence, Lily considered her words with care. "That's very sweet of you, Ian. I'm flattered. But I don't think it would be appropriate."

"Why not?"

"When I come to your hearing and ask them to give you a second chance, it wouldn't look very good if they find out we went on a date."

"You'd do that for me?"

Lily nodded, confirming her decision to both herself and to him. "Yes."

"That would be great. More than I could ever ask."

"If not for the fact that I have a boyfriend," Lily said, "we could have maybe even dated when this was over." Then she realized that in her effort to let him down easy, she had just given him a monster of a mistruth.

Is it a sin to lie if I'm trying to obey God by being nice?

22

BIBLE STUDY HIGHS AND LOWS

For their Bible study on Friday, their numbers had grown. Lily had invited Bree, and she began attending. Madison had invited both Ella and Hannah. Ella had said yes but was a no-show, while Hannah had said no but came anyway. Today they were both there. And Jason had invited Ryan, who had joined them on Thursday. Today Ryan brought Shea.

In less than a week their Bible study had grown from two to eight.

Even though Lily had only been reading and studying the Bible for a few weeks, she was shocked to realize that she already knew more than some of her classmates. She could also explain things to them in a way they could understand, clearer than

Madison and Jason, even though they knew the Bible much better.

"You bring a fresh perspective to it that Jason and I don't have," Madison had told her that morning. "We can all help each other better understand the Bible."

Today's passage covered Jesus turning water into wine at the wedding in Cana. The miracle amazed some of her classmates, but others remained skeptical. Frustrated that some of their group doubted Jesus's abilities, Lily blurted out, "Hey, he's God. He can do anything."

Madison gave her head a quick dip to confirm Lily's insight.

That's when Principal Gardner walked up to their table. He wasn't smiling. Lily held her breath, wondering if they were in trouble. They probably were, though she had no idea why.

"I've received some complaints about your unsanctioned proselytizing," Principal Gardner said.

Lily didn't understand what he meant, but he must mean their Bible study.

"You can't talk about Jesus at school," he said in clarification.

Madison responded. "With all due respect,

we're doing this during our free time, there are no teachers involved, and we're not using any school materials. Plus, everyone who's here wants to be here."

The principal scowled. "You should've run this by me first."

That's when Jason spoke up. "Did the chess club get permission to play chess?" He pointed across the cafeteria to a group of guys involved in intense games of chess. "Or the Dutch Blitz table?" Jason pointed in another direction.

"What about the students playing D&D?" Madison asked.

Principal Gardner raised his eyebrows. "There are students playing Dungeons & Dragons at my school?"

Madison turned to a table on the opposite side of the cafeteria and pointed. "They've been doing it every day for a couple of years."

"I had no idea," he sputtered. "Even so, despite the Equal Access Act, we have a separation of church and state issue to deal with. I must insist that you desist."

Madison looked up at their principal. "Mr. Costner says that separation of church and state isn't in the Constitution. It's not even a law. It's an idea Thomas Jefferson wrote about in a letter to a friend."

"Are you sure about that?"

"Yes," Madison said. "I wrote my government term paper on it. Mr. Costner said it was college-level work."

"I must investigate this," the principal said.

"And the neat thing," Madison added, "is that it wasn't to keep religion out of the government. It was to keep government out of religion." Madison inhaled slowly.

Lily knew Madison was getting ready to say something really important.

"I wonder, sir, if Thomas Jefferson would think that you telling us we can't read the Bible in school violates what he meant by separation of church and state?"

23

A MESSY MEETING

On Saturday, Lily and Madison worked eight-hour shifts at Citrus City. Their plan was to go straight from work to meet Jason's mom at her home. Madison had set it up. She also let Jason know. He'd take his sister, Claudia, to the mall. This would allow Lily and Madison to talk with his mom privately.

But Lily still had no idea what she was supposed to say. Though she kept checking her notebook for an update, no new instructions appeared.

What she did know was that they should pray about it. She looked at Madison, who kept her eyes fixed on the road as she drove. "I think we should pray about our meeting," Lily said.

"Great idea! Go for it."

Lily hadn't expected this.

Usually, Madison took the lead when they prayed. Mostly Lily would agree with her. Only occasionally would Lily add more words to Madison's prayers. "Okay, then. I guess I can do this." Lily folded her hands and closed her eyes. This helped her focus her attention on God. She filled her lungs with air as she waited for the words to form in her mind. At last, they did. "God, help us when we talk to Jason's mom. Tell us what to say and what not to say. Show us when to talk and when to listen. Be with Madison as she leads this, and let me know what I'm supposed to do. I ask this in the name of Jesus the Christ, Amen."

This time it was Madison's turn to agree. She did so with a hearty "Amen" of her own.

Lily opened her eyes and turned to look at her best friend and surrogate sister. So far, they hadn't discussed their plans for the meeting. She knew only that Madison would begin. Anxiety over the unknown agitated her insides.

Again, Lily folded her hands and closed her eyes. She breathed a silent prayer. *Lord, help me calm down. Fill me with peace. Show me what to do. Amen.* She opened her eyes and drew in a slow breath. *Better. Much better.*

All too soon, Madison pulled up to Jason's house and parked at the curb. The girls got out of the car and walked to the front door. Madison rang the doorbell and then stepped back. She smiled and waved at the doorbell camera. Lily did too.

Soon the front door opened. A smiling Mrs. Hayes graciously welcomed them into her home. The aroma of freshly baked cookies filled Lily's nostrils. She licked her lips, anticipating what Mrs. Hayes had made. Until she had moved in with Madison, Lily had never enjoyed freshly baked homemade cookies, something she was getting quite used to.

Lily didn't need to wait long to find out. On the living room coffee table sat a plate of oatmeal cookies and three glasses of milk.

"I didn't think you girls would appreciate tea and crumpets, so I made cookies." Mrs. Hayes gave a nervous laugh, as if realizing her attempt at humor had failed. She motioned toward the couch. Lily and Madison sat as Mrs. Hayes moved to a matching straight-backed chair.

She perched on the seat's edge and looked at Madison. "When you asked to meet, I assumed it was to talk about Jason. But when you indicated

Lily would join us, I was at a loss as to what to expect."

"We do want to talk about Jason." Madison's words came out careful and measured. "And his relationship with his father."

Mrs. Hayes stiffened. "I, for one, do not."

Madison continued. "I have no idea what you went through and the pain he caused, but it's important for Jason to have a relationship with his dad."

"He's an adult now. That's his own business." Unblinking, Mrs. Hayes clamped her lips together. "I, however, want no part of it."

"But he's your son."

"I suspect he'll meet with his father soon enough," Mrs. Hayes said. "But do not expect me to encourage or even condone its occurrence."

"Mrs. Hayes," Madison said with patient gentleness. "Jason has already met with his dad. He's just afraid to tell you."

Mrs. Hayes leaned forward in her chair. She glared at Madison. "And I suppose you had something to do with this."

"I was there, yes," Madison said. "But actually, it was a God thing."

Mrs. Hayes stood. "Ladies, this gathering is

over." With an outstretched arm, she flicked her hand toward the door. "I bid you adieu."

Madison slowly stood, and Lily tentatively followed her example. She glanced at the plate of untouched cookies. She so wanted one, but now was not the time. Even worse, she hadn't said a single thing. She prayed silently, *Help me!*

As the pair walked toward the door, Lily's mind frantically searched for the right words—for any words.

Mrs. Hayes opened the door. "I'm sorry you young ladies wasted your time in coming here."

Lily's chance to say something was about to end. At last the words came to her. As Madison walked through the doorway, Lily stopped.

She looked straight into Mrs. Hayes's eyes. "I don't know who my father is. But I do know that he's a selfish man, doesn't care about me, and has no interest in being part of my life."

Lily blinked, offering a silent prayer that she would not cry. Not now. "When Madison told me that God was my Heavenly Father, my first thought was that I wanted nothing to do with him. I assumed he'd be just like my biological father. I could never trust a God like that."

Lily wiped at her left eye, trying to push back

the tear that was forming. "But then I saw how Madison's dad acted. He was strong but gentle. Also loving. Maybe God was the same way. That was a God I could love. And now I do."

Lily sniffed. "If Jason doesn't have a relationship with his dad, is that going to affect his relationship with God? And what about Claudia? If you told her only bad things about her dad, is she only going to think bad things about God?"

Mrs. Hayes looked away and gulped. Lily turned toward Madison and left as well. The door shut behind them, and the deadbolt slid into place.

By the time they reached the car, the full fury of Lily's tears released. "That couldn't have gone any worse," she sputtered. "Why did God have us do this?"

"I don't know," Madison said. "It wasn't at all what I expected."

"What are you going to tell Jason?"

Lily held her breath as she watched Madison inhale and exhale—twice. Madison pulled out her phone. "I'm going to tell him you gave his mother something to think about."

24

FULLY FAMILY

As they drove home and discussed what happened—and didn't happen, Madison summed it up nicely. "We didn't get what we expected, but we did obey God. I think that's what matters."

"What's that thing you told me about planting seeds?" Lily asked.

"We plant and trust God with the harvest."

"Yes! So it's like we planted a seed in her mind and now it's up to God to make it grow?"

"So right," Madison said. "How'd you get to be so smart?"

Despite her watery eyes, Lily glowed. "It's because I have you and your family to teach me."

When she realized they might have actually accomplished something good, Lily's somber mood lifted.

They arrived home right on time. Dinner awaited. Lily retrieved the check from her backpack that she'd written during break. It was her first rent payment, which was made possible because of her first paycheck from her first job. With her paying token rent, just like Madison, Lily moved one step closer to fully becoming part of the family.

She handed the check to Dad. He studied it. Lily held her breath. This check-writing thing was new to her. *Did I do it wrong?*

But when he smiled, so did she.

"Lily," he said as he rested his hand on her shoulder. "I'm so pleased with the great strides you're making at becoming an adult. This is an important step forward to help you learn financial responsibility. As the father figure in your life, I couldn't be prouder."

His lower lip trembled. A warm satisfaction filled her. Not only did he love her, but he approved. She was in a safe place, with a family that cared for her and nurtured her, both physically and spiritually.

Having completed her instruction to pay rent, the remaining item on her list was adult adoption.

Lily had indeed researched it, at first worried what her biological mother might think. But she soon realized it didn't matter.

Unlike child adoption, which cost a lot of money, took a long time, and didn't always work out, adult adoption was much easier. It was inexpensive, quick, and most always successful.

She liked the idea of being adopted into God's family and had warmed up to the idea of being adopted into the Monroes, but did she have enough nerve to ask?

Lily didn't want to risk losing what she'd already realized by reaching for more than she needed—or could ever hope for. Besides, God hadn't told her to ask them to adopt her, only for her to look into it.

So Lily kept quiet.

When she opened her notebook on Sunday morning seeking clarification, there was none. *God, should I ask them or not?*

She thought about this during church. She continued to ponder it throughout lunch. Then she prayed, asking God what to do. The answer formed in her mind. *Ask them during Sunday afternoon family time.* She was sure it was God speaking to her.

Yet she didn't know what to say. She waited for the right time. And she waited. As their Sunday afternoon family time was ending, Lily stood abruptly and cleared her throat. Three sets of eyes looked up at her, curious and in expectation.

She looked at Madison, then Mom, and Dad last. Fixing her gaze on him, she said, "I have a really important question. But don't feel you have to say yes. Really." She paused as she whispered the shortest prayer possible, *Help!*

Bolstered by supernatural courage, Lily opened her mouth. "Dad. Mom. Will you adopt me?"

Acting as one, all three of the Monroes leapt to their feet and rushed toward her. Arms shot out to pull her in, smothering Lily with the best hug she'd ever had, the best she could ever hope for.

Mom cried.

"This is something we've been talking about," Dad said. "We even have the paperwork filled out and were just waiting for the right time to mention it. Let me get it." Dad extricated himself from their family hug and soon returned, grinning as he waved the paperwork.

"All we need to do," he said to Lily, "is to date it and have you sign it. Oh, and there's one question you need to answer. Do you want to keep your last name or take ours?"

"I'll wait until Michael and I get married before

I change my last name." Lily's eyes popped open in wide-eyed horror. She covered her mouth with both hands. *Did I just say that aloud?*

"We didn't know Michael had discussed his intentions with you," Mom said.

Lily relaxed her tense body. "A girl can always hope."

25

FINAL INSTRUCTIONS

Lily paged through her notebook, marveling at all that God had done in her life. Each instruction brought back memories, some humorous, a few embarrassing, and all affirming in the end. Sometimes she stumbled before succeeding. Other times she succeeded on her first or second try. Through it all, she had learned to obey God. She'd grown closer to him. Her faith had matured. She was also learning to listen to him and hear the words he implanted in her mind.

Lily didn't need her book anymore to hear from her Lord. She knew this for sure. The last instruction on the last page had told her to review everything she'd been through.

She did.

But now, when she turned to the last page again, a new instruction replaced the one she'd just completed.

It said, "Give this book to someone who really needs it."

Her heart soared as she thought of Michael. She would give it to him. Surely God wanted him to have it next. This book would help him just like it had helped her and Madison before her.

"Not Michael," God's words formed in her mind. "Though you have a growing relationship with Michael, this book is not for him. There's someone else who needs it much more, someone who's going through a difficult time, struggling with relationships and questioning his faith."

Lily immediately knew who.

Jason. *I'll give the book to Jason.*

If you enjoyed *The Curious Calling,* please leave a review online. Your review will help others learn about this book and encourage them to read it too.

Thank you.

THE CURIOUS COMMAND: BOOK 3 IN THE CURIOUS GIFT SERIES

CHAPTER 1: LOSING IT

Jason Hayes glared at his mom and stomped from the kitchen. "I'm an adult. And I don't want to go to church anymore." He marched down the hall toward his bedroom, slamming the door as he entered.

Why am I acting like an emotional teenager? he asked himself. *Because I still am one*, he answered.

He flung himself onto his bed and willed himself to cry. He could not. This infuriated him even more. *What's wrong with me? Why am I so upset?*

To others, it seemed everything was going his way. He was about to graduate from high school, on track to be their salutatorian. His dream college had accepted him. Never mind that he had no clue what to study or do with his life after that.

He also had an amazing girlfriend, someone every guy in school would be happy to date. Madison had been there for him when Dad spiraled out of control and they lost their home. Madison had listened and offered encouragement. And she prayed for him too.

Through it all, she became his best friend. Their relationship had grown. This year she became his girlfriend. And though they had never discussed it, he knew they had a future together.

Last, he had reconnected with his father, something he had longed to do for the past five years.

Everything was aligning. *So why am I such a mess?*

An impulse to flee intruded, compelling him to act. He rolled over and jumped off his bed, threw open his bedroom door, and strode down the hall with intention. He grabbed the car keys.

"Where are you going?" Mom asked.

"Out."

"I have work in one hour," Mom said. "Make sure you're back by then."

"No problem."

"And don't leave me with an empty tank."

Jason didn't respond. He didn't care. He just needed to get out of there. Starting the car, he jerked it into drive and punched it. The tires squawked. A tinge of guilt hit him for abusing his mom's car, yet he felt better for it.

He drove, aimless at first, with no destination in mind. Yet Jason soon found himself at a nearby park. It was the nature preserve, a refuge where he and Madison had spent many hours. It had become his sanctuary.

Today he was the only one there. That made sense. It was still early spring. He shivered but didn't care.

It was when walking these trails that he felt closest to God. Yet today he felt nothing. God wasn't there. He was alone. Jason punched the air. Once. Twice. Three times. Aside from releasing a bit of tension, it accomplished nothing else—except to tweak his shoulder.

Not finding God in nature, Jason spun around and retreated. But he didn't return to his car. He plopped onto a picnic table, staring up into the sky. He balled his fists and set his jaw. Wallowing in self-pity, Jason closed his eyes and lost track of time.

The sound of a car brought him back to reality. The thought of someone intruding on his privacy infuriated him. He wanted to be alone.

Whispered voices of two women drew near. At last, they stepped into view. There stood Madison and her best friend, Lily, who held a gift at her side. Jason sat up. He released tension as he blew air from his lungs. He almost smiled.

"Did you forget about meeting us at the coffee shop?" Madison asked.

Jason closed his eyes and sighed. "Sorry."

"We waited for half an hour and got worried. So we decided to come to you."

"It was a good guess that I'd be here," Jason said. "I hope you weren't searching for long."

Madison shrugged. "I just used our tracking app."

When Jason had suggested they get an app so they would always know where each other was, it had seemed like a romantic gesture. But now he realized it was also practical. "I'm glad you did. I'm going through some stuff today."

"So I see," Madison said.

"I'm kind of a mess." Jason bit his lip. "Sorry I forgot to meet you."

"But we're here now," Madison said, "so it's all good."

Jason glanced at the gift in Lily's hand. He didn't want to presume it was for him, but he did anyway. He studied her for clues and then scrutinized Madison.

"Gram left me this when she died," Madison said. "I used it for a while. When I didn't need it anymore, I gave it to Lily. She used it and doesn't need it anymore, either. So now she's giving it to you."

"*We* are giving it to you," Lily clarified.

"No," Madison said. "It was yours to give, and you picked Jason."

"It wouldn't look very good for a girl to give a present to her sister's boyfriend," Lily said.

"So what's it like to suddenly have a new sister?" Jason asked, looking first at Lily and then fixing his gaze on Madison.

"It's the best!" Both girls said it at the same time. They turned to each other and giggled.

Then Lily stepped toward Jason, holding out the present.

In expectation, he took the gift from her. "Thank you. Both of you." He tore into the package.

It was a book with a rugged leather cover, a rich burgundy. Written in bold block letters, the title read, *How to Make a Difference in the Lives of Other People.* Under it was a soft yellow lightning bolt.

"Give it time," Madison said.

"Just be patient," Lily added.

Jason scrunched his eyebrows as he studied each girl to figure out what they meant. He put his thumb on the cover to open it when his phone beeped. "Oh, no! What time is it?" He didn't wait for an answer. "Mom's got to get to work, and I'm late." He jumped off the picnic table and sped to his car. Halfway there, he turned around and, in mid-stride, called out, "Thanks for the book."

ABOUT PETER DEHAAN

Peter DeHaan is an adult who dreams of being a teenager. When he's not contemplating grown-up thoughts, his mind retreats to the domain of invented worlds with his loyal and most real, yet still imaginary, friends. What grand adventures they have: righting wrongs, solving problems, and making their world a better place to live.

His first published adventures came to life in "The Next High Priest Series"—a faith-friendly speculative fiction adventure in a world just like ours . . . only different.

After *The Curious Gift* books will come "The Ice Creamed Series," a present-day quest for friendship and love, all the while trying to survive high school unscathed and ping-ponging between responsible impulses and irresponsible slipups.

Want more? Get a free short story from The Next High Priest Series along with news of upcoming books when you sign up to receive updates at PeterDeHaan.com/fiction.

FICTION BOOKS BY PETER DEHAAN

The Curious Gift Series

The Curious Gift

The Curious Calling

The Curious Command

The Next High Priest Series

Seeking the Sovereign

Confronting the Chaos

Dueling the Devil

Reforming the Religion

Freeing the Prisoners

Fighting the Fanatics

Perfecting the Priesthood

Pursuing the Politicians

Restoring the Repentant

Learn more at PeterDeHaan.com/fiction.

www.ingramcontent.com/pod-product-compliance
Ingram Content Group UK Ltd.
Pitfield, Milton Keynes, MK11 3LW, UK
UKHW040008200726
13854UKWH00001B/98